THE EVOLUTION OF ALICE

DAVID ALEXANDER ROBERTSON

HIGHWATER
PRESS

Canada Council   Conseil des arts
for the Arts   du Canada

We acknowledge the support of the Canada Council for the Arts, which last year invested $157 million to bring the arts to Canadians throughout the country.

Nous remercions le Conseil des arts du Canada de son soutien. L'an dernier, le Conseil a investi 157 millions de dollars pour mettre de l'art dans la vie des Canadiennes et des Canadiens de tout le pays.

HighWater Press gratefully acknowledges the financial support of the Province of Manitoba through the Department of Culture, Heritage, & Tourism and the Manitoba Book Publishing Tax Credit, and the Government of Canada through the Canada Book Fund (CBF), for our publishing activities.

HighWater Press is an imprint of Portage & Main Press.
Printed and bound in Canada by Friesens
Design by Relish New Brand Experience
Cover photo by Pauline Boldt

Print ISBN: 978-1-55379-518-6
Digital ISBN: 978-1-55379-527-8

Library and Archives Canada Cataloguing in Publication

Robertson, David, 1977-, author
    The evolution of Alice / David Robertson.

ISBN 978-1-55379-518-6 (pbk.)

    I. Title.

PS8585.O32115E96 2014   C813'.6   C2014-903935-2

100-318 McDermot Ave.
Winnipeg, MB Canada R3A 0A2
E-mail: books@portageandmainpress.com
Toll-Free: 1-800-667-9673
Fax-Free: 1-866-734-8477
www.highwaterpress.com
www.pandmpress.com

FSC
www.fsc.org
MIX
Paper from
responsible sources
FSC® C016245

to jill

CONTENTS

ONE

The boy, dressed in a too-big black wool suit complete with a poor-boy cap, sat at the edge of the lake throwing large rocks into the water and watching them disappear. His dress shoes, also too big, black socks, and clip-on tie, rested near his bare feet. When tiny waves thrust upon the shore, the boy's discarded clothing was momentarily submerged. He didn't notice, nor would he have cared if he did notice. It wasn't long before an old man navigated his way down the slight embankment, across the shore, to stand beside the boy. The old man wore similar clothing to the boy's, right down to his own poor-boy cap. The old man watched the boy pick up another large rock and toss it into the water.

"Everybody's wondering about you," the old man said.

The boy didn't answer. He picked up an even larger rock and threw it. It splashed hollowly and disappeared.

"Why did you leave?" the old man said.

The boy shrugged. "She felt like an old tire. She didn't feel like Mom. Mom was warm."

The old man smiled on one side of his face and sighed. He placed his hand on the boy's shoulder for a moment, then kneeled down and sifted through the large collection of stones at their feet. Eventually, he picked up a black, flat stone. The boy watched as the old man skipped the stone expertly across the water. It skipped five times before disappearing beneath the surface. The boy was momentarily amazed by the skipping stone but quickly picked up another rock indiscriminately and threw it into the lake. The old man watched the boy do this, then knelt down and carefully selected another rock, black and flat and smooth. The boy looked at the rock resting in the old man's palm.

"You know," the old man said, "my rocks have much more fun than yours."

The old man flicked the rock toward the lake. This time, it skipped six times before sinking. The boy watched after the skipping stone, and kept watching for a moment after the rock had sunk. The boy then shook his head.

"It doesn't matter," the boy said. "They all end up at the bottom of the lake."

"They sure do. Each and every one of them," the old man said. "But, Grandson, sometimes it's how you get there, not where you end up."

The boy walked over to a very large rock and sat down on it. He thought about what his grandpa had said for a long time. The old man came and stood beside the boy. Eventually, the boy lowered his hand and began to search through rocks resting around his feet. He picked up a white stone that was flat and had a little wedge at the corner he felt would fit his thumb just perfect. He held the stone up to his grandpa.

"Would you teach me how to make it skip?" the boy said.

The old man nodded.

NIGHTLIGHT

WHEN THE LITTLE GIRL AWOKE, IT WAS DARK. Darkness on the rez wasn't the same as darkness in the city. In the city, darkness hides within the recesses, away from the warm glow of streetlights, away from the curious glares of porch lights, away from the blinding sheen of cars' headlights, the high beams and the low beams. In the city, the darkness is shy. On the rez, however, in the open spaces, in the absence of artificial lights, the darkness plays. It always scared the little girl. It was where the monsters were—the fiends, the ghouls, the ghosts, and goblins. The girl's mother always turned on the nightlight—a bright little thing that was shaped appropriately like the sun—before putting her to bed. But on this night, when the little girl awoke, the light was off.

She found that her mother was sleeping with her, but this was nothing new. Her mother always slept either with her or on the mattress on the floor with the girl's two big sisters. The little girl instinctively shuffled backwards until her tiny bum was pushed up against her mother's stomach. But the darkness started to play games with the girl. It turned the dresser into a big, hairy ghoul. It turned the toy bin into a white, hovering ghost. It turned her stuffed animals into hungry little goblins. And she swore she saw a fiend, green and grotesque and hungry, stalking back and forth in the hallway just outside her bedroom door, waiting to eat her whole with its large and terrible jaws. She flipped over in bed so she was facing her mother and placed her tiny palm onto her mother's cheek.

"Mommy," she said.

Her mother didn't move.

"Mommy," she said, this time a bit louder.

But still her mother didn't move. She wanted to hide behind her mother, but she was pushed right up against the bedroom wall, so there was nowhere for the little girl to go. She turned back around and peeked out across the bedroom from behind the protection of her mother's arm. The monsters were still there. The little girl knew they wouldn't leave until the light came back. It was the only thing they were afraid of. She decided to do a very brave thing. She shimmied out from underneath her mother's arm and slid off the bed. Her naked feet touched the wood floor, and she ran toward the nightlight in order to turn it back on. Her thin, shoulder-length hair chased behind her, bouncing up and down with each step. She stepped over her sisters, all the way across the room, right up to the electrical outlet. She tried to ignore the scary things behind her, and the fiend waiting for her outside the bedroom, as her tiny fingers fumbled with the nightlight, trying to make it work. She'd seen her mother turn it on many times and knew how to do it, but each time she flicked the nightlight on, it didn't light up.

She ran over to the mattress and tried to wake up her middle sister. The little girl lowered her head so that her face was in front of the middle sister's. Their noses touched.

"Jayney," she said.

Jayne groaned. She swatted at the air, as though a fly was buzzing around her head, and turned over to face the other direction. The little girl tried to wake the big sister up next. She crawled right on top of her sister. She placed her hands on either side of her big sister's head and lowered her face so that it was right in front of her big sister's. Their noses touched.

"Katty," she said.

"What is it?" the big sister said.

"Nigh ligh," the little girl said.

Kathy turned over, tossing the little girl down onto the mattress. She buried her face into the pillow.

"Turn it on," Kathy said, her voice muffled by the pillow. "Turn on the nightlight then."

The little girl sat up on the mattress and crawled over to Kathy.

"It's broked," she said.

"Go to sleep," Kathy said.

The little girl tried to wake Kathy again, but it was no use. She was alone.

She looked around the room from her sisters' mattress. The monsters were bigger now, and getting closer. The little girl thought her only chance was to be braver still and run out of the bedroom to try and find light. Otherwise, the monsters would get bigger and closer until they caught her. She got up from the mattress, ran out of the bedroom and into the hallway. She didn't break stride. The light was out there, somewhere. She ran down the hallway as fast as she could. She swore she could hear the tip-tap-tip-tap of the fiend and its awful high heels chasing after her. She shrieked as she made it out of the hallway. She ran straight through the kitchen and living room and out the front door.

When she got outside, she looked back at the house to see if any of the monsters had followed her there. It was just as dark outside as it was inside. She looked around. The things she recognized in the light were far different in the dark. The toys strewn about the driveway, the ones she played with in the day, were things she wouldn't go near in the night's long shadow. Everything was ready to pounce on her. Her lower lip jutted out, and tears began to well up in her eyes. She wanted her mommy, but she was too afraid to go back inside the house. She looked around, desperate for something that might help. She started at the house and

5

methodically turned clockwise, her tiny feet shuffling against the gravel as though slow dancing with the night. She could hardly see the highway and wouldn't go there anyway. Her mother wouldn't let her near it in the day, and she certainly wouldn't go near it in the dark. The shed at the end of the driveway looked like a haunted house, and the little girl quickly looked away from it. That left only one place.

The little girl looked past the swing set, which was a giant crawling spider; past the big old tree, which was a spooky giant, and the tire swing hanging from it, which was a lasso the giant would use to catch her; past the field, which, during the day, was one of the safest places the little girl knew, where she played hide-and-seek with her sisters and nobody could ever find her because the tall grass was higher than she was; and there, at the distant tree line, she saw a bright orange light flickering behind the trees as though the sun had gotten stuck on its journey below the horizon. She was sure this was the place for her to go, where the darkness would disappear, and with it the monsters. And she thought it would be safe to walk there, too, because in the field she was the best hider, and even the darkness and its playthings wouldn't be able to find her.

The little girl made her way behind the house, past the swing set and the big old tree with its hanging swing, and disappeared into the field's long wispy grass. She felt safer there, even though it did seem darker because the night sky was partially hidden behind the bowing blades of grass. There was a great distance between the house and the tree line, and with the girl's little feet and little legs and little steps, the distance felt even greater. But she kept walking. Every once in a while she heard rustling behind her and was sure the monsters were after her, but she was equally sure they could not find her. She pushed blade after blade away from her as she walked farther and farther, and blade after blade whipped against her skin as she got closer and closer. Finally, the little girl emerged from the field of grass and stood before the tree line.

She was happy to be greeted by warmth and light. The tiny ball of orange the little girl had seen from the driveway was revealed to be a large fire, the flames dancing to a symphony of cracks and pops, and dressed in warm colours—reds and oranges and yellows. The sharp beats coming from the fire was the sweetest rhythm she'd heard. She walked into the trees. The farther in she got, the brighter the light became, and soon the monsters were a distant memory. They did not dare follow her. And perhaps they could not. Perhaps they were lost somewhere in the field along with the disappointed darkness, still looking for her in the deep grass. The only hint of the darkness was now the trees' shadows as she walked closer to the fire. And when she stepped into a clearing the darkness was gone entirely.

As though drawn by the warmth and the light and the comforting sounds, the crackling and popping, like a lullaby, the girl kept walking toward the fire until her toes began to burn. She just might have walked right into the fire, too, if a man hadn't come running from the other side of the blaze to stop her.

"Hey there!" the man said.

The little girl stopped. The man ran up to her, picked her up, and brought her away to a safe distance. When the man put her down, she looked him over carefully. He was familiar to her; the dirty blue jeans and soiled white T-shirt, the thick legs and thick arms, the broad shoulders, the square jaw, the clear blue eyes, and the bright yellow hair. The man seemed to glow in the fire's light, as though he was a part of it. The little girl smiled at him.

"Hi!" she said.

The man laughed.

"Hi there, little one," he said.

He crouched down in front of the little girl. He reached over and touched her on the nose with a quick poke. He even made a sound like a doorbell. The little girl laughed.

"You know," the man said, "you're not supposed to be here."

The little girl's face quickly turned into a frown. Her lower lip stuck out and her arms crunched against her sides. Her mother would have been familiar with this position. She was about to cry.

"Buh my nigh ligh's broked," the little girl said with a shaky voice.

The man gathered the little girl into his arms, picked her up, and shushed her gently. She placed her head against his chest along with one tiny palm and disappeared in his embrace.

"Now listen," the man said, "I made this fire just for you, you know that?"

"Yup," the little girl said, gasping for breath as she forced back tears.

"It's just, well, you've come far too early," the man said.

The little girl could hold back tears no longer. And if the light hadn't scared away the darkness, her sobs certainly did.

"I need my nigh ligh," she said.

"Okay, okay," the man said, and gently patted her back. He did this until her breath evened out, until the tears stopped coming.

"I'll tell you what," he said. "I will build this fire so big and so bright you will be able to see it all the way from your house. Would you like that?"

"Yup," the little girl said.

"Okay," the man said.

They stayed there for a moment, the little girl in the man's arms, and the man gently rocking her back and forth, back and forth. He made sounds like the ocean from his lips, and she stared deep into the fire. Then, as the warmth showered over her, as the cracking and snapping serenaded her, as the light kept her safely removed from the darkness and its monsters, her eyelids grew heavy. She blinked once, twice, three times, and fell asleep.

The little girl woke up again in the night. She found herself tucked into an afghan on the couch in the living room, the one she always sat on when her mother let her watch her favourite television shows. She was afraid at first, as her eyes adjusted. She was worried it would be dark again, and she would have to run away from the ghouls and ghosts and goblins and fiends. But she found the darkness was shy, hiding from a steady glow coming in through the living room window. The little girl got up and walked to the edge of the couch. She crawled up onto the armrest, went on her tiptoes, and looked out the window. She smiled when she saw, past the swing set, past the big old tree and its hanging tire swing, across the field she played hide and seek in with her sisters, a bright orange light burning behind the tree line that coloured the sky like the dawn. She watched the light for a long time, her eyes wide with wonder. Eventually, she climbed back down from the armrest, walked back across the couch, and snuggled down underneath the afghan.

TWO

Matthew had just finished his first tour through the rez. It wasn't anywhere he thought he'd ever be. He'd just found out he was part Cree, and that he had distant relatives, including a cousin, living there. All the same, he was fascinated by the experience. His parents hadn't ever been there either, and the lot of them, in their Chevy Traverse, spent about an hour driving all around the area. Matthew had been assigned a Culture In a Box project for his grade-three class back in the city, and had been alerted to his Cree heritage by his parents, albeit a bit reluctantly. It turned out that he was far more interested in being Cree than he was in being Scottish.

After finding out he was Cree, he had asked his father, innocently, "Daddy, am I related to the homeless people?"

His father had chuckled and said, "Oh, I don't think so, son."

Matthew took notes throughout the excursion through the rez. As twilight hit and they were on their way back to the city, he read them.

"Houses here don't have street addresses; they have broken cars. I bet people find their way around by looking for types of broken cars. There are nice things in ditches. I saw a tricycle and a car tire and a lawn chair. They all looked in pretty good condition. The front yards look fun. There are trampolines and toys and four-wheelers. I saw an old man with no shoes out front of his house carving a wooden boot. I think I'll like being Cree."

Matthew smiled at his notes. His teacher had said in his report card that he had exquisite handwriting.

THE EVOLUTION OF ALICE

Alice lived in a converted trailer about thirty feet off the highway, a few kilometres into the rez. If you visited her, you'd see a bunch of kids' toys in the driveway. A toy car that her toddler, Grace, could push herself around in with her little feet, just like the Flintstones; a plastic basketball net about three feet high with a few balls lying around it, one of which couldn't fit through the hoop and caused Grace fits; a rickety metal hockey net with mesh like a damaged spider web and a few floor hockey sticks resting on top of it; and a turtle-shaped sandbox full of beach sand from the nearby lake and digging toys and trucks and buckets. You'd see her home, that old trailer, and notice she didn't have real curtains on the windows, but instead hung blankets—homemade blackout blinds, she'd say. On the kitchen window hung a majestic wolf, on her bedroom window a soaring eagle, and on the kids' window a big smiling Dora. There were a few large buckets by the front door for gathering water from the lake. A few feet from the trailer you'd see a little green shed which housed more toys, some tools she never used, and a lawn mower that she did. A few feet still from there you'd see the outhouse, and there was nothing much to describe about that, and you wouldn't want me to anyway.

If you went around back, you'd see a swing set that used to be red but was now pink from all the sun. The girls liked that it was pink. Some of the plastic had cracked on the seats, but the swings still went high, and the slide still sent the kids bouncing off along the ground. Near that, tied to a big overhanging branch on what she figured was the oldest tree on the whole rez, you'd find a tire swing. It was a big, old tire, worn bald, that was attached to that branch by strong yellow twine. If you went back there at most times of the day, you might see Alice on that swing, rocking back and forth, sometimes really high, always watching her girls play in the big open field that stretched way back until it fell off into the horizon. She used to tell me that back there, on the swing, was her favourite place to be because she could see forever, and no matter how far away her girls got, she always knew exactly where they were. And if she went really high, she said she felt closer to heaven. She told me being on that old tire swing was better than praying ever was.

Inside, Alice kept a good house for what she had. The first room you'd be in is the kitchen, where there was a sink with a faucet that was just there to tease her, because water didn't come out of it. She did the dishes in there, though, so it wasn't all that useless. Her cupboards were half full of stuff she'd rather not have fed her girls, but on the money she was getting the cheaper stuff was all she could manage, and the cheap stuff was junk. In the fridge the most important things were the eggs and bacon, small indulgences she allowed herself. It was for a good cause, though, because every morning, no matter what, no matter how late she'd been up, she got up with her girls, sat them down, and cooked them up two strips of bacon each and two over-easy eggs. She'd sit there and watch them eat, and when they smiled she managed to smile and that made it a good morning.

The living room was just off the kitchen. There wasn't much to it. She had an old television set and a few channels, most importantly PBS, where she could throw on morning cartoons for the girls, educational type shows, nothing like Sponge Bob or Power Rangers. Beside the television there was a stack of about 10 Dora

VHSs, and they were good too, for learning Spanish and all that. She didn't like the kids sitting in front of that old television too much, they were mostly outside anyway, but from time to time it was good to fire it up and let them get babysat by the thing so she could have some rest. She'd fall asleep on the hide-a-bed, and it happened often enough that the sound of Dora's voice was like relaxation music to her. Dora counting to ten in Spanish was like counting sheep jumping over the moon.

Down the hallway you'd come to Alice's room, where there was a twin mattress on the floor with a comforter draped over top of it, and a dresser by the back wall. She didn't have a closet or anywhere to hang things up in because she didn't wear dresses or blouses, never needed to. Next door, the kids' room was done up as girly as possible. The two oldest girls, Kathy and Jayne, they slept on a queen mattress that had a princess comforter, and Grace had a Dora one, of course. Grace was the only person in the house who had an actual bed, a white captain's bunk with a fancy headboard and everything. The other girls were okay with it. Everybody in the house doted on Grace. There was a Rubbermaid bin in the corner of the room filled with toys; Barbie and My Little Pony and Littlest Pet Shop and Dora were all in there. If she spent frivolously on anything, it'd be toys I guess, because she wanted her girls to have fun, to feel like girls. They shared one big dresser, and each girl had two drawers. They shared a bookshelf, too, and it was full of books she'd gotten in town at the library when they sold off their old stock. There were always good ones in there. In some ways it was Alice's room, too, because often instead of sleeping in her own bed she'd crawl into one of the girls' beds and cuddle right up to them.

And that was Alice's house. The only other thing you need to know is something you might have already guessed. Alice, she loved her girls more than anything. For Alice, it didn't really seem like there was too much else to love, so she just threw all her love at them. I'm a friend of hers, me. Name's Gideon. The kids call me uncle on account of me being there so much, ever since they were born, and before that too, really. If you went to visit Alice, chances are I was there, too; standing beside Alice as she swung back and forth, both of us watching her beautiful girls, watching them forever in that big field; getting right into the sandbox with them, filling my shoes up with sand and not caring one bit; slam dunking the balls into the basket on their heads for fun, and easing air out of the big ball when Grace got frustrated, just so she could fit it through the rim; eating bacon and eggs with them at the breakfast table when I'd slept over with Alice, cuddling up to her in bed just like she'd cuddled up to her girls. Sometimes adults need a cuddle too, you know.

So, this story I'm going to tell you, it's about Alice, and other things, too, but I'll let you figure all the other stuff out. Stories mean different things to different people, so who'm I to tell you what you're going to learn from me? You'll learn what you'll learn, and maybe you'll learn nothing, and that's okay too. But now that you can picture it, just for a second close your eyes and walk down the driveway. Kick away some of those toys if they're in your way, come inside, and sit down at the kitchen table. That's where it all starts.

The day before it happened, well, Alice told me it was just like any other day. Had she known, maybe she would've taken more time to savour things, like you do with a good bite of food or a nice cold beer on a hot day. You let it sit there in your mouth for as long as you can to try and remember the taste, the texture, the temperature. I'm guessing she would've stayed a bit longer at the table during breakfast, watching her girls eat the food she'd made, them savouring the bacon as she savoured them, taking snapshots of their faces with her mind, ones that never faded, just got a little frayed at the edges with time, like a wallet photograph. They all smiled like she did, big and unabashed. Alice knew their smiles well. Those things, they weren't hard to remember. But sometimes the joy they gave to her in those moments, well, that was what she wanted to keep forever, locked away somewhere deep inside her chest. They smiled more than she did. But kids, they didn't worry like adults did. I'm guessing she would have talked a bit longer to them, too. Because the girls had some good things to say about life, she could've stood to hear a bit longer, so it really sunk in. Well they say hindsight's 20/20, and all that means is you shoulda known then what you know now. It's a real piss-off, that's about it.

She got up before the girls, just like she always did, and cooked them up their bacon and over-easy eggs. Typically, the smell woke those girls up, and the sounds, too. The pop and crackle of the cooking bacon was like an alarm clock. They came out of the bedroom rubbing their eyes, their pyjamas still on, their hair all nappy, their little bare feet making soft kissing sounds as they walked across the linoleum floor. One by one they plunked down at the table, and one by one they said good morning to their mommy.

"Good morning, my darlings," she said back.

When Alice put their plates out in front of them, their talking stopped for a little while. The only sound in the house was their mouths chewing up their breakfast—tiny lips smacking and tiny teeth grinding—and the news report from the television set, which Alice usually had on in the morning while she made their meal. During breakfast, she'd alternate between watching her girls eat and watching what was going on in that big world outside the rez. Sometimes it seemed like another world altogether. Sometimes it just made her feel small. The girls took peeks at the television, too, even though Alice didn't like them to, not to watch the news anyway. She thought there were always too many bad things going on and they didn't need to bother themselves with it because they grew up seeing enough bad things. Kathy, the oldest one, glanced over at the TV just in time to see the end of one particular news story about a robbery gone wrong, and to an adult it was a bit funny to see the storekeeper jump over the counter and lay a beating on the would-be thief. To a kid, it was one guy hitting another, and to most kids, seeing something like that wasn't too familiar. To Kathy, though, seeing something like that was all too real, on account of their family history, on account of what she'd already been through right there at home. She jerked her head back quick, and Alice noticed, too, because she flicked off that program as fast as you could imagine, like an old west gunslinger in a high-noon standoff.

"You okay, Kathy?" she said.

Kathy didn't say anything at first. Instead, she looked right down at her plate and made a picture out of the spilled egg yolks. Alice didn't want to push, so she sat there and waited. The other girls kept on eating, oblivious that something was going on with their sister, enjoying their protein. When Alice watched Grace pick up her little pink plate and lick the yolk off, she only chuckled. Usually, Grace's antics brought something a bit heartier out of her. But the other girls, they didn't remember much from before. Not even Jayne, who was around four or five back then. They were lucky that way. Kathy, she was a fun girl, a happy one too, but every once in a while you'd catch her looking off at empty spaces, her eyes big and sad. Finally, Kathy placed her fork down, rested her cheek against her hand, and took a long, deep breath.

"Is Daddy ever coming back?"

Alice stopped eating too. It wasn't something they'd ever talked about. It wasn't something Kathy had ever asked before. She knew where her ex was, about two hours away at Stony Mountain Penitentiary, and chances were, he wasn't coming back from there for a while yet. He wasn't one to get time off for good behaviour is what I'm trying to say. But it didn't seem as simple as that, either. He'd get out some day. He'd probably try to shoulder his way back into their lives in some way, but not by being with Alice again. No. I think that sweet talk had worked too many times. She'd taken him back, he'd promised not to hit her any more, and then pretty soon he'd be laying hands on her again, bruising her up real good, like a cut apple left out on a countertop. If he did show up, though, just what would she do? What would he do? Alice told me thoughts like that were the ones she kept way down inside, deep enough to ignore, deep enough that she could pretend they didn't exist. She said that sometimes she went all day without thinking of him. But when she did think of him, those were hard times. When she did, it was usually at night, alone in her bed, and she'd steal off into the dark and find her way into her girls' bedroom, lying down beside one of them and spooning them real tight. A girl Kathy's age didn't need those kinds of questions, and she didn't need to worry about the *whens* and *what ifs*. In the end, Alice decided on a simple answer, for the time being at least. There'd come a day where the girl might want to go visit her old man, if even just to yell at him or ask him why. That'd be a hard day, and those would bring the hard questions, the hard answers.

"No, Kathy, he ain't coming back," she said.

Kathy kept her head pushed right up against her fist for a good long while, and then finally lifted it back up and brought her dishes to the sink. She was good like that, always helping out around the house without being asked. She'd done that lots of times when Alice was in her bedroom curled up into a ball, shaking and scared, and that asshole had stormed off to get some air. She'd tidy up the living room or put away the toys, something to help her mom out. Jayne, she'd follow suit. She always did. She looked up to Kathy quite a bit. Grace, well, she was too young to remember anything. Alice liked to think she was the pure one, the baby who'd never be able to recall the anger and violence. Alice loved that about her. Her joy was real joy, untouched, without reservation or pretension. In that moment, Alice wanted to make

Kathy feel good. She didn't do that enough. There were never enough I love yous, never enough hugs or kisses.

"You were always such a brave girl," Alice said as Kathy went to grab Grace's plate.

Jayne picked up her own plate to bring it over to the sink.

"What do you mean?" Kathy said.

"You know, when Daddy got angry. You were always so smart, taking your little sisters and locking yourselves up in the bathroom. You're a good girl."

Kathy stopped in the middle of the kitchen, Grace's plate still in her hands. She looked confused. Her head even tilted like a little puppy dog, and it would've been cute if it wasn't such a sad topic.

"But, Mommy, I didn't go there by myself. That man took me."

"What man?" Alice said.

"Your friend," she said.

It all seemed so matter-of-fact to Kathy. She didn't understand why her mom was acting so odd, why her skin turned pale, why she looked like she was about to faint. Jayne knew it, too. She was standing beside Kathy at this point, nodding her head up and down. Grace was nodding, too, because she copied everything the others did, said whatever they said, went wherever they went. Most of the time, this was a good thing. She already knew her alphabet and could sing "You Are My Sunshine," in key even. But then, she also went off outside without telling her mom sometimes, just like the older ones did. Alice had to watch herself, too, because if she ever let a profanity slip by her lips, there was Grace saying that same word about twenty times in a row just like she was reciting her ABCs.

"What friend are you talking about?" Alice said.

"Wha fend?" Grace said.

"The big man with the blond hair," Kathy said, shaking her head in disbelief that her mom could forget such a thing. She continued, "He took us to the bathroom. He'd come hold our hands and bring us there, and then he'd lock the door."

"Lock tha doh!" Grace said.

"Yeah, Mommy," Jayne said.

"Yeah, whenever Daddy started shouting, every time," Kathy said, "and then you'd come get us after, remember?"

"And just where exactly did my friend go?" Alice said with a tone that challenged her little ones, but Kathy and Jayne, they were sure that that man was with them just as sure as they were that they'd eaten breakfast. They looked at each other and exchanged shrugs.

"I don't know. I guess he just left," Kathy said.

The girls stood there as Alice sat quietly in her seat, letting it sink in, processing what the girls had said and wondering if their imaginations had run wild. She asked them about her friend, what he looked like, and it was all general stuff. He was a big man, broad shoulders and jaw, short blond hair, and wore regular clothing—blue jeans and T-shirt kind of outfit. That was an eyebrow-raiser for Alice, because if the man was what she thought he was, he'd be wearing a white robe and wings. Then again, maybe that'd be too scary for a child. Maybe he had to fit in.

She told me it reminded her of a car ride she had taken with her mother years before, when she was a teenager—before her kids, before the beatings. It was late and they were heading back home from town. The sky was perfectly clear and the stars were bright and countless, twinkling like snow did in the sun. On the horizon, they could see the northern lights, that familiar glow, the waves of colour shimmying across the sky like flowing ribbons. Then those ribbons started collapsing to the middle of the sky, right at the end of the highway, until they formed what looked like a face. Alice thought she had to be seeing things, so she asked her mother about it, but she saw it too. They pulled over and watched it until the ribbons spread out again and it was like the face was never there. She'd always thought it'd been an angel. Had that angel come back to help protect her most precious things?

She took another long look at her girls. They'd lied to her before. Daily, in fact. Kids lied all the time. Did you climb up onto the counter and eat the sugar? No. Did you pull your sister's hair? No. Did you take Mommy's makeup? No. But with one look from Alice, the noes always became meek, guilty yeses. Always. But she knew the noes were lies before the girls admitted it. She could tell by their faces. And the girls didn't have those faces on that morning, standing there innocently, wondering why their mommy didn't seem to know her own friend was helping them. It was too much to think about. Her mother had raised Alice in the church, but none of that really stuck. Alice, she was never sure if there was a God or not but usually decided that there wasn't. Figured if there were a God, she wouldn't have the life she did. I mean, she was happy about her girls, I already said that, but not all the other shit—growing up without a dad, losing her mom like she did, gettin' beat on by Ryan. Yeah, Alice was always pretty sure there was no God, but now maybe not, maybe He'd been there all along.

She had the girls get dressed and followed them out to the back yard, where they went off to play, and she climbed up onto her tire and began to swing as high as she could. That's when I came by. I always checked the back yard first, because more often than not, that's exactly where they were. I saw the girls way out in the field, playing tag or hide-and-seek or some game like that, and walked up to Alice, and we exchanged greetings bit by bit each time she swung by me. That's how I found out about what happened that morning, in bits and pieces, each time she passed by.

"You believe in God, Gideon?"

"Why?"

Then she'd be gone, up in the air. On her way down, there was another exchange.

"My girls saw an angel, you know."

"What? When?"

Up, then down.

"When Ryan was beating on me."

"How?"

Up again, then back down, and all I pretty much did was recite "when, what, why, and how" as she said all she wanted to say.

It was a long conversation to have that way, but as I heard more and more I wasn't about to ask her to come down from the tire swing. Up there, she was safe, and the girls were safe and that was that. After she told me everything, she stopped pumping her legs, and after a few minutes her swinging settled into a light rocking. Made our visit a lot easier. I saw her struggling with it a bit, her brain that is. So I decided to say something all Elder-like to her. I pointed to an old dirt road just about 20 yards to our right. It was pretty much grown over with grass, you could hardly see it, but it was still a road. It went right through the field, right up to the distant tree line, and got tinier and tinier on its way.

"You know, my grandpa used to tell me that all the roads around here just lead us right back home," I said.

I wasn't even sure what the connection was, and after I'd said it I kind of felt dumb about it. I tried to figure what I was getting at, for Alice and for me, so I added, "But, I don't know, maybe he was wrong, maybe roads take us to where we're s'posed to be."

Alice crunched her eyebrows up and looked at me funny. "Are we talking about real roads, or pretend ones? Like ... figurative roads?" she said.

She knew those big words from all the reading she did. Lots of books, she read. I didn't read much, me, but I knew that word from my grandpa, so I said, "Figurative ones. Like, the paths we take in life."

"I don't know. I think your grandpa was right." She paused, then added, "Anyway, just because they saw a man doesn't mean they weren't imagining it. You know? They don't have to lie about that if they thought they saw somebody. You ever had an imaginary friend?"

"Not one that locked me in a bathroom away from that jerk-off boyfriend of yours," I said. I meant it, too. I knew her ex, and he was a piece of work. The day he got hauled away was a good day, and I wasn't the only one who thought that. "But, if they've got an angel lookin' over their shoulders, it's not anything to worry about, is it?"

"I guess not," she said.

We stood there in silence for a few minutes. She was looking out across the field at her girls, watching as their heads bounced in and out of view from the long grass. But I could tell her mind was somewhere else, and I didn't have any other brilliant things to say to make things better.

"I'm glad my mom is dead, in a way. At least today I am," she said, "because she'd have my ass in church in a second."

"Well, maybe that isn't such a bad idea, you know."

She shook her head and patted the tire like it was a faithful ol' dog.

"I got my church right here," she said.

I wasn't about to argue with her about that. Even gave the tire a pat, too. I left her there to go and do my own things. She invited me over that night and I promised I'd try to make it back to see her. I didn't see her until the morning, though. I'd like to tell you it was for something important, that I was doing something meaningful and just couldn't go, but the truth is I fell asleep on the couch watching one of them *Law and Order* shows. I'll probably always think about how I screwed up like that. I remember before I fell asleep I was thinking about that old road and what I was trying to say to Alice. I guess I was just saying she shoulda been happy right where she was, because those girls, they were beautiful little things and they loved their mommy so much. She felt bad for a long time after her ex was taken away because she'd kept him around too long, but she did her best, I think. It's hard letting go of people you love, whether they deserve your love or not. It doesn't matter what I was trying to say anyway. All that mattered is I wasn't at Alice's place and I damn well shoulda been.

Like I said, the next morning I went to check up on how she was doing, and to have a bite of that breakfast she always made for the girls. If I was being honest with you, and I ain't been nothing but honest so far, I'd tell you that I loved being there at the kitchen table eating bacon and eggs just as much as the girls did. My house, well, there wasn't ever much to do there. It never felt like a home, just somewhere I put my head down at night. Alice's house, with her girls and the comfort I felt there, it was more like a home to me. I could almost smell those strips of bacon cooking on the stove before I could even see her place. As I approached her house, though, I could see something was wrong, and those smells, well, they weren't ever going to mean the same thing to me.

There were cars in her driveway, and they weren't rez cars, either. There was a cop car and an ambulance, and when I saw that my stomach dropped. Felt like pulling over and puking right on the side of the road. As I got closer, I could see a white sheet on the ground and a mound of something underneath it that looked like a pile of snow. My heart began to beat out of my chest. There were people gathered around out front of Alice's door. I parked on the highway, just beside her driveway, and ran up to the house. When Alice saw me, she fell right into my arms, sobbing and wailing like I never saw her do before. She pulled me right down to the ground with her, and I kind of leaned up against the trailer and cradled her in my arms like a baby. Her body shook and she got my t-shirt all wet with her tears. The whole time I couldn't stop staring at the sheet, guessing at its size and asking myself who could be underneath it. There were two local constables there—I knew both of them, Ernie mostly, because he and my grandpa were pretty good friends—and some paramedics. All of them just looked down at us all serious and sad, and I kept myself from asking what happened for the longest time. I guess not hearing it from anybody made whatever happened not real, like if I stayed on the ground forever I could just close my eyes and get stuck right there in time.

"She's gone, she's gone," Alice said.

Her words were muffled because her face was right up against my shirt, but I heard them well enough.

"Who's gone?" I said, even though I was scared about the answer.

She didn't say anything more, just the same two words over and over again, each time getting quieter and quieter, until those words were barely a whisper. About then, scared or not, I felt like I'd had enough and needed to know for my own sanity, because my brain was racing all over the place. For the first time, I looked away from the mound, the white sheet, and met eyes with Ernie. I asked him without saying a word, just by motioning with my eyes to the sheet. I swear that sheet is always going to haunt me, just like a ghost. He told me all quiet, as though if he said it soft enough Alice wouldn't hear it, relive it, all over again. I don't think it mattered, though. I think by that time Alice had shut herself off from the world. She was whimpering into my shirt in short little gasps of air, like kids do when they can't shut off the tears. Ernie said that, the night before, Alice fell asleep on the couch sometime after supper. At some point, little Grace crawled out of bed and went out into the driveway for some reason, maybe to try and dunk the big ball into the hoop. A car pulled into the driveway and hit her, ran right over her. Maybe its headlights weren't working. Maybe the driver wasn't paying attention. Whatever the case, as soon as Grace was hit, the car peeled away quick and left Grace lying in the driveway. Still alive. Struggling to breathe, maybe trying to move, trying to get home, where she was safe no matter what. I hate thinking of her like that. Dying alone, dying scared, crying out for somebody to come help her, crying for her mommy. God damn it. The paramedics said she suffered for a long time until she died early in the morning.

If the car had stopped and let somebody know, Grace probably could've been saved. Instead, she was gone, just like Alice said; the baby, the pure one who would never remember the violence the rest of 'em might never forget. Ernie said he didn't know who could've done something like that, but he wouldn't rest until he figured it out. I trusted him about that. Ernie was a good man and he never lied to me about nothing. To be honest, thinking about who'd done it wasn't really on my mind at that point. I just kept thinking about poor little Grace. Always felt like I was really her uncle, not just a pretend one. Always felt like she was my little girl. I rested my eyes on the white sheet one last time before they took her away. I imagined the sheet was bundled up there on top of her bed, that she was snuggled underneath it, warm and safe. Then, I looked away and buried my face into Alice's hair to blind myself.

"I'm sorry," I said.

After the paramedics left with Grace's body, I helped Alice to her bedroom and tucked her tight into her bed. She fell asleep instantly. That's the thing about tragedy and sadness: it's like running a marathon—sucks the life right out of you. By that time she had nothing left, and her body just turned off. I knelt down and sat at her bedside for a little while, watching her sleep, hoping she would have a dreamless sleep, because dreams were sure to turn to nightmares. Even dreams about Grace would, because dreams were tricky. When you're in them sometimes you think they're real. When you wake up, you realize they weren't. I didn't want her to think Grace was still there. Waking up to find she wasn't would've been too much hurt for Alice. There was just us and the silence and that was nice, even during all the hurt. Sometimes pain needed a quiet place to be, to spread out and get less sharp, I guess. I ended up staying with Alice 'til the afternoon, thankful for her eagle towel, because it left her room pretty close to pitch black, and she slept for a long time.

Now, the other girls, Kathy and Jayne, they'd been taken away from the chaos by Alice's sister, Olive. She lived just across the way. But by the time I left Alice's room and went to look out the living-room window, the girls were back, playing way out in the field as though they were trying to get away from it all. Olive was standing at the swing set watching them. The girls didn't look any different from a distance. They were still bobbing their heads up and down, playing tag or hide-and-seek. Maybe they were pretending Grace was just hiding somewhere in the tall grass, they could never find her anyway. Everybody deals with tragedy in different ways, whether they realize it or not. Kids do too. Olive, she was standing there and holding herself steady with one hand on the swing set, her shoulders slumped. Every once in a while I saw her body kind of shudder a bit, holding back tears I guess. But stopping tears was like trying to catch rain. They were going to come; you just never knew when they would.

I hadn't cried yet, me. I wanted to, though, real bad, now that Alice was sleeping and I was alone in her trailer. I even tried to find ways to make myself cry, because I had lots of tears for little Grace. I walked down the hallway and went into the girls' bedroom. On the dresser by Grace's bed there was a framed photograph of Grace, Jayne, Kathy, and Alice—in that order—crouched down behind the house. I recognized the field. I scanned their faces, especially Grace's, and noticed how much they all looked like Alice. Their eyes, their hair, their mouths, their skin colour, everything was just like her. Seeing each of those girls' faces was like looking at Alice when she was young: Alice at ten, Alice at five, Alice at two. It was like one of those evolutionary charts at school. Those girls, they were going to be pretty, just like Alice. They'd have soft cheeks, big brown eyes, beautiful black flowing hair, thin gentle lips, and perfect olive skin. Grace, she would've been so pretty, a real princess.

I stared right at her face, right into her eyes, and knew that she'd be stuck just like she was right there in the picture, forever a girl, forever innocent. And that made me feel a bit better, because we all get damaged in one way or another. Grace, she wouldn't. Crouched there beside her sisters and her mom, her mouth stretching wide as it could get, smiling as big as I ever saw it, that's how Grace would be remembered, how she'd always be. I put the photograph down and looked down at Grace's bed. Her sheets were bunched up in a mound, just how she left them last night before she went outside to do whatever she was doing. My eyes flashed to the driveway, to the sheet formed around her tiny frame, and that bit of good feeling I had went away fast. I felt like my chest was on fire. I rushed out of the house, down the driveway, and back into my car. I rolled down the window and peeled right out of there.

Best thing I could think about doin' was driving as far away from there as I could get, like doin' that could get me farther away from the memories and emotions. So I drove somewhere big and flat and wide open, where I could see the horizon, where the road kept going and going until it disappeared right into the end of the world. Then I started to look for the northern lights, to see if I could see what Alice saw when she was younger. I wanted to know that Grace went somewhere good after all the pain she went through. But I didn't see shit. If there was a God and He did have little Grace, I guess He wasn't about to tell me about it. Nah, he was set on making me work for that kind of faith. Grandpa says nothing is worth it if you don't have to work for it and I guess he was right about that. People always talk about going to a better place, and I had to find a way to be okay with that. Besides, anywhere had to be a better place than where she was, dyin' like she did. I looked up at the sky. Without the northern lights it was all black and endless, and I figured at worst Grace was seeing something just like I was, and that wasn't too bad, neither.

The next evening, I found myself back at Alice's. I parked along the highway. Didn't think I'd ever be able to drive right up to her house again. When I arrived, the sun was well into setting, and there were warm colours everywhere, like autumn, and it was like all those orange and red hues everywhere were trying to flush out the cold death left on everybody, on everything. I walked up to the house, and then around back just like I'd always done, and was surprised to find Alice swinging on her tire swing, going as high as I ever seen her. The girls were out in the field, their heads dipping up and down in the long grass like buoys on a lake. I walked over to the tree and didn't say a word, just stood there and watched Alice swing until she was ready to stop. I followed her with my eyes so she didn't seem like such a blur, and when her face became clear I could see her cheeks were soaked with tears and sweat. She was pumping her legs hard, and the tire swing, well, it was getting up so high that I got worried Alice was going to fall outta there. Each time she got up to the highest point, the rope would go slack for a second, and I could just picture her falling to the ground, but then the rope snapped tight again and she came racing back towards me, and each time I breathed a sigh of relief.

When she came to rest, I guess I waited for her to say something because the words weren't coming to me. I wasn't sure what I'd say other than sorry a million times over. What do you say to someone when their child dies? Especially when somebody could've done something about it. Alice could've stayed awake. I could've stayed awake too, shown up like I said I was going to. Best I could do now, though, was put my hand on her shoulder and let her say whatever she wanted to, whenever she wanted to. It took her a long time. She just kept staring out into the field, watching her daughters like she always did, from time to time searching as though Grace might just pop into view. When somebody dies, you keep thinking you're going to see 'em, like they'll just walk right into the room like they always had. But Grace's head wasn't poppin' out of nowhere, and eventually one little tear came falling out of Alice's eye. She wiped it away and took a deep breath, then she turned to me, and her eyes almost broke my heart right there.

"Why didn't he save her?" she said.

And then more tears joined the one little one, and she began to sob all over again, keeling over in the tire swing, causing it to rock a bit back and forth as though it knew to try and comfort her. She meant the angel of course, the one that had brought her kids to the bathroom and locked the door to get them away from Ryan, to protect them. It was a fair question. The strange man who came before wasn't there in the driveway that night, didn't bother to take Grace's hand and lead her out of the path of the car that hit her. For whatever reason, he let her get run over, and there didn't seem to be any good explanation for it. But maybe people weren't supposed to understand things like that. I wanted to say something comforting to her, but anything I could think of was going to make her sadder, or more hurt. "She'll live on inside you." "Your little angel's with all the other angels now." Those would've been bullshit words to say.

"You'll see her again," I said eventually, because with the talk recently about the angel her girls saw, and what Alice saw as a teenager, it seemed like there could've been something out there, even though it had just screwed up pretty royally. (I say could've been because I still wasn't sure myself. To me, you never really know about something unless you put your own eyes on it). She motioned out toward the field and shook her head. She looked defeated, empty.

"I can't see her now," she said. "That's what matters."

"Well," I said, "she's just a little thing, you know. Just keep looking if you have to."

"Would you do me a favour, Gideon?" she said all blankly, like she was talking to me in her head, like I wasn't really there.

"Of course I would," I said.

"Could you come by tomorrow morning to make the girls some breakfast? They need to have their breakfast. Olive can't cook. She burns the bacon and she makes the yolks hard. Can you do that?"

"Yeah, Al, I can do that."

She thanked me then turned away, back toward her girls, towards the field that seemed bigger and emptier now, and started to pump her legs again to get up as high as she could go. And me, she left me behind, way back down there on earth, watching her soar just like the eagle on the blanket in her bedroom, the one she made into a curtain. From where I was, I could pretend she was carefree like that, when her face was out of view, anyway. And that made me feel good, too, for the times she was close to heaven. I didn't think there was anything more I could do right then, didn't have any deep thoughts about roads or any shit like that. And Alice, she probably didn't want to talk any more anyway. Sometimes people just want to be sad and alone. So I left her like that, pumping her legs, swinging up high in her tire swing, her girls bouncing up and down in the field, and Grace hiding somewhere nobody could find her, somewhere safe.

THREE

Kathy was missing. Gideon had been driving for more than an hour looking for her, scanning the forested areas on either side of the highway for her, getting out and checking for footprints, shouting her name as loud as he could, both while driving and when stopped. But he was yet to see anything. He could still hear Alice's voice when he'd arrived that morning for breakfast. Desperate. Terrified.

"Find her, Gideon! You have to find her!" she'd cried.

He said that he would, but as each minute passed with no sign of Kathy, the grip on his steering wheel had grown tighter. He'd seen the news about Aboriginal girls who had gone missing. It wouldn't take much for somebody to pick her up, take her away. And then she'd be gone forever, like Grace.

It was on his third pass on a stretch of highway that Gideon noticed a turtle in the middle of the road. He passed it at first, thinking, rightly, that there were more important things to do. But even so, against his better judgment, he glanced into his rear-view mirror at the turtle he'd passed and imagined a vehicle running over the poor thing. He couldn't stand the thought of it. He stopped the truck, got out, and walked over to the small, dark green mound. He watched as it crept along its way, oblivious to the danger it was in, then leaned over and picked it up.

It felt strange in his hands, hard like plastic but warm and smooth, and he marvelled at its design, how the different-sized shapes, squares, and hexagons fit together like a completed jigsaw puzzle. It was far too beautiful to be destroyed. Gideon brought it to the side of the highway with its head tucked inside its shell, and looked around for a good place to let it go. There was a stream alongside the road, and it seemed as good a spot as any. He navigated his way down the embankment; then, careful not to fall into the running water, he reached forward, submerged it beneath the surface, and let it go.

The turtle darted off with all the agility of a fish, sharply moving from left to right on the way as though dancing in its freedom. He never thought a turtle capable of that. He laughed, and watched the thing swim all the way downstream until it was out of sight.

ANCHORAGE

DOWN HIGHWAY 57, and with nothing to worry about aside from the slight curves and undulations along the neglected road ahead, Edward pressed down on the gas pedal and watched as the speedometer's red needle crept past 160 km/h. He made sure to keep an eye out for the RCMP, as well as oncoming motorists, but the few times he had been down the same road had yielded little, if any, traffic, so this was a small concern. The bulk of his attention thus rested on the area directly in front of him. He curled his hands around the steering wheel and felt the soft material compress under his fingers. Occasionally he snapped his head left or right and then back to the front again, and when he did this he thought the sight of landscape rushing past his vehicle was pretty, like a pastel painting of the actual scenery. He wished, in certain moments, he could somehow freeze time and better appreciate the view rather than glimpse it in such short bursts.

His was a two-and-a-half-hour trip and didn't require too much "luggage." That is to say, he didn't have much more with him other than the shirt on his back, a few road snacks—including a ham sandwich he was reticent about eating—and, on the passenger seat, being treated very much like precious cargo, a Nikon camera. The Nikon D600, to be exact, which held a prominent place in their family, particularly adored by Nicky, who cherished it on the level of a well-behaved dog. Edward had seriously considered strapping it in with the seatbelt. Besides that, he'd brought his iPhone, which was currently hooked up to the car's stereo via an auxiliary cable and playing all the songs he normally couldn't play when Nicky was in the vehicle (rock music with what she called *whiney* lead singers).

It was at this point that the phone rang, cutting out the music and replacing it with the ringtone selected for Nicky's calls: "piano riff." He rolled his eyes, not so much at the fact that it was Nicky calling, but more so that he had been enjoying the music—Thom Yorke was whining away on "Reckoner"—and hated to have it interrupted.

"Hey," he said.

"Hi. Where are you?" she said.

"Honestly, I don't even know where I am. I'm officially nowhere."

"How long until you get there?"

"About thirty miles," he said.

Nicole paused, and Edward wasn't sure why until she said, "Just how fast have you been driving, Edward?"

He realized that during the brief silence she'd calculated his speed based on when he'd left and how far he had to go. She was good.

"There's nobody around, hon. I figured I could cut time off the trip," he said, then added, melodically, "so I could get home to you sooner."

A pronounced sigh was followed by Nicole saying, "Just be careful, you don't have to go exactly the speed limit, just not, you know, a million kilometres …"

Abruptly, he heard a familiar two beeps through the speakers, which meant the call had been dropped. Thom Yorke cut back in, and Edward was thrilled to hear him. He glanced down at the iPhone, saw there were no bars, and realized he was on a stretch of road where the cell phone connection was tenuous at best. He remembered the area and figured the reception would remain like this. Why would there be good reception in the first place? Who even drove in this area? He'd asked similar questions the last time he'd been through these parts with Nicole, when they were on their way to Jeff's funeral. Edward had wondered why Jeff wanted to get buried in such a secluded area. To Edward, people who got buried in places like that either didn't like anybody or thought nobody liked them, plain and simple. Nicole had rolled her eyes. "Or you just like the quiet," she'd said. That could've been it, too. Lord knows, there was nothing but quiet out there.

He settled into the comforts of the road: the long stretch of highway with its languid curves, the white-noise lullaby of the rubber tires against asphalt and the accompanying, pleasantly soothing vibrations, and the promise of the horizon, how it appeared close enough to catch but never got closer. It made Edward feel as though the trip could be infinite. Then, suddenly, his iPhone notified him of two missed calls and a voice-mail message. The voice mail played back as follows: "Ed, it's me, I know you probably lost service, but you also could've run off the road or something, which I shouldn't be telling you, of course, considering your tendency to ... well, never mind ... crap ... could you just call me as soon as you can?" He dialled Nicky and, as the phone rang, slowed to a compromising speed of 110 km/h.

"Hello?" she said upon answering the phone.

"Considering my what, exactly?" he said, but knew damn well she was about to talk about his "problem."

"All I meant was that I didn't *intend* to give you anything more to worry about, because..."

"Because I worry about everything."

"Well, you do. You *know* you do."

"I do not worry about *everything*," he said. He did worry about many things, but certainly not every single thing he could potentially worry about.

"Okay, Ed, have you finished your ham sandwich yet?"

"My ham ... no, but it's not even lunch."

"It's five after one."

He checked his clock, and mouthed "damn it" when he saw that she was correct, to the minute even: 1:05 PM.

"You know lunch isn't *only* at noon. People do eat at different times."

"Oh, God. It's so *insanely* difficult to prove the smallest point with you, even when you *know* I'm right."

"Hon, you know luncheon meat is good for like, 93 seconds after you buy it, right? You know how my stomach's been."

"Yes, I know how your stomach's been, and I know, also, the specialist said he thought your stomach was fine aside from needing Tums once in a while."

"Zantac, actually."

"Ed, *fuck*. Ever since Jeff died. No. Ever since Jeff got sick, this has been a *thing*. You are like a damn illness chameleon. Somebody's got a brain tumour and you've all of a sudden got a massive headache. You are an *illness chameleon*. You have to be cognizant of..."

And then, as though he was owed some cosmic favour, the cell service cut out again, and he was reintroduced to his music playlist. The red needle slowly began to creep back up, but not a shade past 110 km/h. Sometimes, Edward thought, he didn't want to talk to Nicole at all. For a moment, he wished the highway went on forever and he could just drive and drive farther and farther out so there'd never be reception. But this thought was gone as quickly as it arrived. He tried to imagine what it would be like to talk to Nicole for the last time, and hoped it wasn't the talk he'd just had with her, because he was, admittedly, now a little worried about going off the road just like she had mentioned. What would he say to her? What profound things would they discuss? How would they say goodbye?

It made Edward think about the last time he'd talked to Jeff. It was near autumn, and he and Nicole had just sat down for supper when the phone rang.

"How are you doing?" Edward had said, and cringed at the words. But what do you say to somebody who is dying?

"I'm okay," Jeff said in a shaky, weak voice that sounded nothing like the Jeff Edward knew.

"I'm sorry about what's happened," Edward said, and noticed Nicky point at herself, so he added, "Nicky is too. What a thing, you know."

"Thanks," Jeff said, his voice nearly a whisper, "but I'm okay, really. I'm at peace with it."

Edward wanted to ask how the hell he could have been at peace with it, seeing as how every health care practitioner he'd seen—naturopaths, homeopaths, gastroenterologists, and so on— had clearly screwed up. Edward never did understand how they all could've missed a tumour the size of a baseball growing in Jeff's stomach.

"Well, you're a better man than I am," Edward said.

"No, I'm not. I just have something you don't."

"Even now, you're trying to get me to believe in God," Edward laughed. "Come on. I mean, *come on.*"

Edward thought back on how he and Jeff had become close in the first place, because they weren't at first, he being Nicole's uncle, and a bit of an odd bird, wearing train conductor caps for no reason and doing other inexplicable things. Jeff had dragged Edward to a church men's retreat one year, and, after Edward surprised himself by having a good time with Jeff, he'd agreed to go back subsequent years. He was certain that he came to know Jeff much better during the retreats but was far less certain he'd come to know God.

"Everybody needs something to keep them safe and secure," Jeff said. "What do you have to lose?"

"Nothing, Jeff."

Nothing. That's what was out there with Jeff. Could God be bothered to be somewhere so damn boring? As Edward rounded a gentle curve, he glanced over at the Nikon camera, ensuring that it remained in place, and repeated the one task he had been given before setting out on his journey. He was supposed to take a lot of good pictures. Nicole and Grandma wanted to see how the trees were growing. Trees. They were saplings. But he supposed that he'd misspoken, even if it had been just to himself. There was nothing *and* a pair of saplings. That was far more accurate, and God probably still didn't give a shit.

Then his thoughts were interrupted as "piano riff" played from his phone. He answered, and Nicky continued with their conversation as though there had been no interruption.

"You're aware of it, aren't you? That you take on other people's illnesses and, like, create the symptoms? Before Jeff got sick it was your head, and before your head it was your heart. People are actually sick, Ed. You know that, don't you?"

"I still have my headache, actually."

"And do tumours last seven years?"

"I don't actually know the answer to that. Maybe benign ones do."

"Edward, you only have one common symptom, and that's *worry.* You're at least aware of *that,* aren't you?"

"Yes," he said, in an attempt to end the topic right there.

"Well, anyway, it doesn't do anybody any good. Not you or me or anybody, to worry like that. Have you eaten your sandwich?"

"No."

"Please eat the sandwich, Ed. Okay?"

"Okay, I'll eat the sandwich."

"Fine, that'll have to do. And don't forget to take the pictures, please."

He looked at the camera and nodded his head as though she could see him.

"Take some pictures from different angles, too, just to see what works best."

"I should have brought a wind machine."

"Ha. You know, it's real pretty out there. Take some of the whole cemetery, too. Wouldn't it be nice to get buried out there one day?"

"I don't want to get buried at all. You know I'm claustrophobic."

"Ed, I swear…"

As Nicky started to talk, Edward noticed something on the opposite side of the road ahead.

"Is that?" he said.

"Is that what?" she said.

"Hang on," he said.

As he got closer, he could see it was a young girl, alone, dressed in a light jacket and blue jeans, and a pillowcase full of something hanging over her left shoulder. She was walking toward him. He pulled over to the side of the road when he was directly across from her and stopped the car.

"Honey, there's a little girl out here. What do I do?"

"A little girl, like a little *girl*? Or a teenager?"

"Like, a little girl. Like nine or ten or something."

By this time the girl had stopped walking and was staring over at Edward. He rolled down his window and rested his arm on the door.

As casually as he could, he said, "Hey there, what are you doing?"

The girl didn't respond. She pushed her hair away from her forehead and placed her bag on the ground.

"Ed, what is she doing?" Nicole said.

"I don't know," he said. "She's just standing there."

"Did she say anything?"

"No, she didn't say anything. She's staring at me," he said.

"Say something else. She's probably nervous."

"Hey," he said to the girl. "How you doing?"

"Edward, don't talk like The Fonz! God!" Nicole said.

Regardless of how he talked, the girl didn't do anything. She kept standing and staring, her pillowcase resting at her ankles.

"I think I'm going to go," Edward said as his foot began to ease off the brake.

He waved at the girl very deliberately, as though he was testing if she was blind. No response.

"Edward!" Nicole said. "You can't just leave her there. Where are you?"

Edward looked around. Trees upon trees lined the highway as far as the eye could see. He didn't think there was anything where they were.

"Nowhere," he said.

"Is there a house nearby? Is there *anything* nearby? Where'd she come from?" she said.

"There's nothing. I told you. I don't know where she came from," he said.

"Well you can't just leave her there, Ed. You can't just leave her *nowhere*."

"What do you want me to do then? Whatever I do she's going to think I'm some kind of pervert."

"Get out of the car and just walk up to her, slowly," she said, and then added, "but keep your distance, though."

"Yeah?" he said.

"Yes, Ed, some monster could pick her up. You have to see if you can bring her to her home."

"Okay, okay," Edward said as he shut his car off.

"Ed!" Nicole said before Edward hung up. "Just take it easy with her, okay, because she might think *you're* a monster, you know?"

"I'll talk to you later," he said.

He hung up the phone and then, deliberately, very un-monster-like, opened the driver-side door and stepped out of the car.

"Hello," he said, staying right where he was, the two of them standing on opposite sides of the road. "I'm Edward. Ed."

The girl shuffled her feet, looked right then left, and shyly put her right hand on her left forearm.

"I'm Kathy," she said.

"How are you, Kathy?" Edward said, trying his best not to sound like The Fonz.

"I'm okay I guess," she said.

"You know," he said, "if you're going to walk on one side of the road, it's better to walk on the side where cars are driving *toward* you, so you can see them coming. It's safer."

"How will I ever get a ride if the cars going my way are on the other side of the road?"

"Good point," he said, "but maybe getting rides with strangers isn't the best idea to begin with."

"Nobody I *know* is going to drive me where I want to go," she said.

"Strangers might not drive you where you want to go either, Kathy," he said.

Kathy picked up her bag and started to walk away in a huff.

"I have a long way to walk, then," she said.

Edward thought of letting the girl go but could imagine what Nicole would say when he talked to her next.

"Wait," he said.

Kathy stopped. She turned around.

"Where are you headed? The city?" he said.

"Alaska," she said.

"Alaska? Where in Alaska are you headed?"

Kathy put her bag back onto the gravel at the side of the highway.

"I don't really know for sure. It doesn't matter, though. When I get there I'm going to go farther and farther."

Edward looked both ways, as though it were necessary.

"Can I come across?" he said.

Kathy nodded. Edward walked across the highway and soon was standing beside the girl. He looked carefully at the pillowcase at her feet and tried to guess what was in it, what a 10-year-old girl would pack. He'd seen fuller pillowcases on Halloween; there couldn't have been much in it.

"What's in there?" he said, motioning to the bag.

"Just stuff I'll need. I got some extra clothes, a book, my toothbrush, and a couple of oatmeal bars."

"Did you bring toothpaste?"

She thought about it for a moment, and, with a disappointed look, shook her head.

"What about water? You're going to need water if you're going to be walking very far."

"Not really," she said. "I mean, no."

"Ahhh, well, travelling 101 is, you bring water and toothpaste. What's in Alaska?"

"A cousin of mine."

"Okay. Here's what I think you should do, and this is just a suggestion. Why don't I bring you back home, you can get water and toothpaste, and *then* we can talk about going to Alaska, if you still want to. Have you gone very far from home?"

"I don't really know. I've been walking for a while."

"Isn't anybody looking for you? Do your parents know you're gone?"

"My mom would hardly notice," she said very quietly.

"What about your dad?" he said.

"If I would've seen my mom or my *uncle* coming I would've hid anyway. They would've just got all mad."

"If you were my daughter, or my niece, I might be mad if you were gone, too, you know," he said.

"I guess so," she said.

They stood there at the side of the highway in silence. Kathy looked to the right for a long time, down the highway, as though she could see all the way to Alaska. Then, she looked to the left, and Edward could see she was already homesick, despite how badly she wanted to get where she was going.

"Do you know the way home?" he said.

She nodded.

"Can I drive you there? It won't take very long in the car I bet."

Kathy didn't take long to decide. She nodded her head again. They walked over to Edward's vehicle. He went around to the passenger side, opened the door for Kathy, and instructed her to place the camera (very carefully) in the back seat to make room, which she did. When she got into the vehicle, he closed the door and breathed a sigh of relief before hopping around to the other side and getting into the vehicle himself. Once more, he was on the highway, this time going even slower, around 85 km/h.

"Do you mind if I ask you why you're planning on going to Alaska? I mean, if it's not just to visit your cousin," Edward said.

She thought about it for a moment.

"The other day my cousin called, and I picked up the phone because my mom was sleeping in the other room. We were talking about how everybody was doing, because my cousin has lots of family where I live, and then he asked me what I was having for breakfast. I told him I wasn't having breakfast because it was after noon and I'd just finished lunch. He said he was silly because he forgot about the time difference."

"Okay," Edward said, and this was followed by a long silence. Then Kathy said, as though Edward hadn't understood her, "Well *that's* why I want to go to Alaska, and then even farther. My cousin said the more west you got the earlier in the day it got. So I'm going to keep walking and walking until it's yesterday, and then last week, and then a few weeks ago."

"Ahh, I see. You think … I mean, you want to go back in time."

"Yeah, I want to go back in time. Not too far, but far enough. I just got to figure out how far I have to go."

Edward hesitated to explain time zones to Kathy because he had an awful feeling that by doing so he would essentially be telling her there was no Santa Claus. But, maybe that was the only way he could convince her not to go back onto the highway all by herself. Even if her mom and her uncle were home when they got there, Kathy might just leave another time, back on her journey to Alaska.

"Kathy, there are different places in the world that have different times. Some times are earlier than ours, and some times are later than ours."

"So, you can go to the future too?"

"No, no. What I mean is whether or not it's 12 o'clock here and nine o'clock over in Alaska, it's the same *time* everywhere. Like, everything's happening *now*. You can't go back in time."

"I don't understand," she said, but her face held the slightest hint of desperation, which meant, to Edward, she did understand, mostly, and simply didn't *want* to understand. He wondered what could be so important that she'd want to go back in time, but decided it wasn't his place to ask, especially now, as she looked sadder by the moment.

"What's happened has happened and nobody can change it," he ended up saying.

"Oh," she said, and turned her head away to look out the window.

"You know, there are things I want to change. I think anybody would want to change something, if they could."

"What do you want to change?" she said as she turned back toward Edward, where he could see a few wet lines down her cheeks from tears.

"I'm on my way to visit a friend of mine who died, and I wish he didn't die. I wish I could go back and, I don't know, help him."

"That's sad," she said.

"Yeah, it is. But, I can't go back. So, I'm going there to visit him and remember things about him I liked."

"I want to help somebody, too," she said.

"Hmmm. Are there things you can remember about that somebody? Things you liked?"

She nodded her head, and right there, Edward could tell she was thinking about those things because a tiny smile presented itself.

"It's right up here, turn right," she said.

Edward nodded, and when the time came, turned right. They drove through some more forested area before the trees cleared to reveal a large open space, where in the distance there were houses visible.

"Do you ever worry about dying?" Kathy said.

"Oh, not really," he said.

"I do. I worry about it lots."

"Lots of people do. You know, I have this person I talk to from time to time when I'm worried, and he's really smart. You know what he tells me?"

"What?"

"He says worry has never changed anything for the better."

This was followed by quiet, and Edward began to think about the words he'd just spoken. It felt like he'd been talking to himself. He knew very well he worried about almost everything under the sun, and that worry had brought him to the doctor's office for everything from headaches all the way to stomachaches. But he was never actually sick. At the height of Nicole's frustration with Edward's anxiety, she'd said, "If there *is* something wrong with you, do you want to spend the rest of your time worrying about it?" He got annoyed at her then but now began to see what she'd meant.

They kept driving, and as the houses got closer he recognized they were on a First Nations reserve. It wasn't what he thought a reserve would look like, but he wasn't sure what he expected. More desolation, maybe—a bunch of boarded-up houses, sad looking people, casinos. The houses weren't the nicest he'd ever seen; they looked quickly built and more like large sheds than homesteads, but, somehow, they were welcoming and warm, and he liked how things just lay unattended in yards, seemingly without a worry about theft. He saw trampolines, toys, quads, golf clubs, and many other things. You'd never see something like that in the city. Finally, just a couple of kilometres from the highway, Kathy said they'd arrived at her home. "Home" was a trailer with an enormous tree directly behind it. A tire swing hung from the tree's largest branch, and a big open field past the tree stretched back forever, all the way to a tree line visible on the horizon. Edward pulled up alongside a line of large rocks blocking the driveway from the road and turned off the engine.

"Thanks for the ride," Kathy said as she got out of the car.

Edward got out of the car too and thought it was best to walk her up to the door.

"You think you can do that? Stop worrying?" Edward said.

"I can if you can," she said.

They arrived at the door and Kathy walked inside. Instantly, Edward heard a cry from inside the house. Not wanting to intrude, he quietly shimmied over a few feet to look. He saw that a woman, undoubtedly Kathy's mom, had buried the girl deep within her arms. Another girl, a few years younger, dressed just like a Disney princess, was standing beside the two of them, crying like everybody else, trying to find a way inside the prolonged embrace, eventually collapsing on top of them. A man was there too, standing in the kitchen, and he noticed Edward outside the front door. He stepped outside the trailer.

"Where'd you find her?" he said.

Understandably, he sounded distrustful.

"Oh, just up the highway," Edward said, and noticed the man's interrogative look, so decided to be more specific. "I don't know, about seven or eight kilometres away?"

"Yeah? That far, eh? And where were you headed?" the man said.

"I was on my way to the cemetery just a little ways from here. You know the one?"

"There're a lot of cemeteries around here."

"Look," Edward said, "I get it. You don't know me from Adam."

"That's right," the man said, "and that's our little girl in there."

"She mentioned an uncle, I guess that'd be you?"

"That'd be me. That's what they call me, anyway."

"Okay, I just wanted to help. She was looking pretty lost out there, and, this might sound strange because we've established that you don't know me, but I couldn't stand thinking of her getting picked up by some creep."

The man thought about it for a moment. He looked back at the group hug going on inside the trailer then turned back to Edward. He stared at Edward for a long time, as though sizing him up. It made Edward feel a bit sheepish, even though he knew he'd done nothing wrong. In fact, he was sure he'd done just the opposite. He gave the man a half grin and tried to look as trustworthy as possible.

"I'm not a creep," Edward added for the sake of clarification.

Finally, the man nodded.

"I guess I should thank you for bringing her home, then," he said. "I couldn't find her, me. Drove up and down the highway for a while. Must've been hidin' on me or something."

"I'm happy to help," Edward said.

"So she was just walking down the highway?" the man said.

"Yeah, she was walking down the highway. Uhhh, said she was headed to Alaska?"

"Alaska, eh?"

"Yeah, she thought she could go back in time. Time zones, you know. Kids sometimes get confused by them."

At that, the man shook his head. Edward could see the same sadness on the man he'd seen on Kathy.

"God damn it," the man said. "Ain't that the thing."

"Why'd she want to do that? Go back in time?"

"Few weeks back, her little sister got run over and killed, right here in the driveway. Just like that."

"That's awful," Edward said.

"Yeah, it's been pretty awful. Been hard on her, you know. Hard on the whole family," the man said.

"They ever find out who did it? Who ran her over?" Edward said.

"Nah," the man said, "and I don't think they're gonna neither. All we know is that the car had four wheels."

"That must make things harder."

"Maybe it did at first, but now I think we're all just trying to heal, you know? Trying not to think about that shit."

"I don't think I'd get over that," Edward said. "Not knowing."

"Well, none of that's gonna bring her back. You just gotta keep living as best you can without her, and hope she's somewhere better than here."

Less than half an hour later, Edward pulled off the highway into a side road leading up to the cemetery. He parked in front of an old-fashioned white church, complete with a roof shaped like a triangle and a steeple at the front that thrust a small white cross into the heavens. It looked under-used, or even abandoned, judging by the long grass growing up against the cracked steps leading to the front door, which was hanging precariously by one hinge. Still, the church was a pretty little thing and gave off a certain aura particular to churches, whether you believed in what they were built for or not.

A delicate fence enclosed the cemetery. It was composed of wood posts and wire and a small metal gate Edward pushed open to enter. Since he'd been there last, there were no new residents at the place—still only Jeff's headstone, which was nearest to the gate, and another, older, headstone near the back corner, the two almost as far away from each other as you could get. They weren't exactly keeping each other company. In the opposite corner to the other headstone, there was a large pine tree, the only mature tree on the lot, which, Edward learned during Jeff's burial, had been planted by Jeff himself years earlier. At either side of Jeff's headstone there were two saplings that would one day mature and become tall pine trees, like guards standing over him. Nicky and her grandma, who had planted the new trees, would be pleased to know they were growing fine.

Over the next several minutes Edward spent time snapping pictures of everything in front of him; the church, the mature pine tree, the fence, Jeff's headstone, and, of course, the two saplings (which enjoyed the bulk of Edward's attention, posing nicely like two models). All told, he took about 50 pictures and, after scanning through them, was quite proud of the quality. He decided some of the pictures might look nice hanging on a wall.

After putting the camera away, Edward went and stood beside Jeff's headstone. He didn't say anything. He was certain people often said lovely things when visiting headstones, but, truthfully, he thought doing so felt a bit silly. He thought if Jeff was anywhere, he certainly wasn't in the cemetery, even though it was a nice, peaceful location, much more appealing than Edward had originally thought for a final resting place. All he did, in the end, was silently wish that Jeff continued to be in a place where he was safe and secure, just where Jeff had hoped everybody should be. He thought of Kathy in that moment, too, and wished the same thing for her, and the little sister she had lost. He imagined Kathy in a cemetery somewhere, standing in front of her little sister's headstone. He never found out how young the little girl was. Edward took a deep breath and tried to fight back a tear that had welled up in his eye. At least, he thought, Jeff had lived a relatively long life, far longer than that little girl. He thought about what he'd said to Kathy, that she should focus on the good things. He hoped she could do that. God knew it was hard enough for a grown man.

Soon, he was travelling back down Highway 57, his music playing through the car's speakers and the cruise control set to a reasonable 105 km/h. He picked up his ham sandwich and considered taking a bite. It was, after all, well past lunch.

FOUR

Gideon stood with Kathy and Jayne at the front of the community hall. They needed to have the funeral in there because almost the whole rez had shown up and the church wasn't big enough. All the people were sitting quietly behind Gideon and the girls, and the only sounds were the odd sniffling and baby crying. Alice was behind them too, sitting there with three empty chairs beside her. Gideon had tried to convince her to come up with them, but she wouldn't. She said it was too hard. She said that, the last time she'd seen Grace, her little baby was beautiful, smiling and alive. At no point had she asked to see Grace's body, and Gideon understood why. He thought Alice probably had perfect memories of Grace and didn't want the bad ones taking over the good ones. He did wonder, though, if she was one of the people sniffling behind them. Maybe she'd used up all her tears. All he'd seen her do today was stare blankly at nothing, somewhere over the casket, as though there was something to be seen against the cream-coloured back wall, like a slide show of cute baby pictures. He'd seen that done before.

Jayne said the casket was so small it looked like a doll's bed. Gideon agreed. Kathy said that Grace looked prettier than she'd ever seen her. Alice had chosen the most beautiful dress she could find, even though she didn't want to look at it, now that it was on Grace. Gideon said that he thought she looked real pretty, although her beautiful olive skin was paler now, as though covered lightly with baby powder. He thought Grace, lying peacefully within the tiny casket, was a perfect-sized doll for the little bed.

REMEMBER SATURN

J AYNE USED TO DREAM ABOUT BEING A PRINCESS, like Cinderella or Sleeping Beauty. She'd wear these cute little princess dresses and spin so hard in 'em that the bottom of the dress rose up into a perfect circle. I always told her she looked like Saturn when she did that, what with that ring spinnin' around her middle. She used to smile so big that her face got all scrunched together, and, when I watched her little bare feet go up on tiptoes and take little steps in little circles, my face would get all scrunched up too. Grace was too young to care about princesses and all that. She used to wear the same kind of dresses only because Jayne wore 'em. She woulda worn blue if that's what Jayne was wearing. She never cared too much about what Kathy wore; I guess there was an attraction for the one closer to her age. Jayne liked that about Grace. Made her feel special. She always used to call her "my baby" like Grace was all hers, and Grace, in turn, always called Jayne "my Jayney." Point is, ever since Grace died, Jayne might've still worn her princess stuff, but she never spun around so pretty any more.

Of course that wasn't the only thing that had changed since Grace died. Things were unsteady at Alice's trailer. It's like when you throw a big rock into the lake and the water ripples for a while before everything's calm again. The bigger the rock, the longer it takes the water to calm down. Well, little Grace dying was about the biggest rock you could imagine. A boulder. One of the things that happened on account of Grace dying like she did was that Alice stopped letting her girls go out much at all, and never without her. Hell, she never even let them out with me, and before that I used to go out and play with them all the time. So the girls were stuck inside, and they seemed all overcrowded with sadness, whether they realized it or not. It was like claustrophobia or whatever, only it wasn't walls crushing the girls, it was memories. Watching TV, those girls were sitting right where Grace used to sit, where she used to bug 'em and crawl all over 'em. In the bedroom, playing with their toys, the girls were always in the shadow of where Grace used to play or sitting beside Grace's bed.

After Grace died I made a point of coming to Alice's place more often than I used to, and that's pretty often, because I used to come to Alice's place more than I was at my own place. I liked being over there, so it wasn't much of a chore, you know. But it was also a conscious effort for me, because, as much as Alice loved her girls, she just couldn't bring herself to do much with them. If the girls were watching Dora in front of the television, Alice would find her way to her room, or Grace's bed, and curl up and read or cry, depending on her mood, and, if the girls were playing in their room, Alice'd be in front of the television watching the news or something. I don't know why that was. Me, I'd've kept those girls shut tight in my arms forever, if I were her. Maybe she didn't want to get too close to them in case she lost another one. Hell, Kathy'd run off the previous week and Alice just about had a heart attack. So I don't think anybody could blame her for that.

Well, anyway, on the day I'm talking about I got over to Alice's house about mid-morning. I parked on the highway, just like I always did since Grace died. Truth is, I didn't have much of a choice anyway, because Alice, she'd made a barricade so nobody could drive up to her house ever again. One by one, she'd taken big rocks from the beach and brought them to the mouth of her driveway, and one by one the barricade got bigger and bigger, until it was big enough to block the whole entrance. I walked around the rocks and made my way to the front door, but stopped before gettin' there because outside the girls' bedroom window there was a big pile of clumsily made paper airplanes. I didn't think nothin' of it right then, other than it was something I never saw either of the girls do before. I just chuckled at the pile and shook my head a bit, even picked one of them up and tried to make it fly, but it sort of just shot right down to the ground nose first. I had half a mind to pick them up and toss them in the trash, because eventually the wind was going to take them all over the rez, flying like they shoulda been in the first place, but I thought better of it.

When I got inside, I saw the girls must've been playing in their room because Alice was sitting all quiet on the couch, watching a talk show; one of those Jerry Springer bullshit shows where there's more shouting than talking. I always thought they shoulda called shows like that shout shows as opposed to talk shows. Anything coulda been on though, because Alice, I don't think she was really watching the TV. I think it was more, like, distracting her. She was real quiet all the time. You know, she must've had lots of thoughts up in her head, unpleasant ones and all that, ones she'd rather not be thinking. The only problem I saw with watching a stupid show like the one she was watching was it didn't require much thinking so it couldn't have been much of a distraction. She woulda been better off watching one of those crime shows I liked. At least those made you use your brain from time to time.

I went over to sit beside her for a little bit, even though I knew there wasn't much going to come of it. We'd developed a routine, Alice and me. I'd say a bunch of things to her, she wouldn't really answer, and then I'd leave her be and go off and hang out with Kathy and Jayne. Those two said lots of things. I didn't hold nothin' against Alice, of course, because Grace's death was still pretty recent and she was dealing with stuff the way she had to deal with stuff. The girls, they were dealing with stuff too, but while Alice was pushing everyone and everything away, the girls were keeping things real close to them, and they sure did love their Uncle Gideon those days. And as terrible as the reasons were for that, I kind of liked being needed like that. Maybe I needed to keep things close, too, because I sure did love little Grace, and the closer I kept Kathy and Jayne to me the less guilty I felt about flaking out on Alice the night Grace died. Yeah, Grace was a boulder for me too, that was for sure.

First thing I noticed when I sat down was a cigarette on the coffee table in front of the couch, resting on a piece of aluminum foil shaped like an ashtray. She'd already sucked half of it back, and I watched the smoke rise from it for a few seconds, appreciating how smoke from a cigarette was maybe the only thing pretty about smoking, how it kinda danced and curled in the air. I didn't know what to think about Alice smoking, because it wasn't something I'd ever seen her do. That's probably why I never said anything for a little bit—I was processing and all that. Eventually, though, I tore my eyes away from the cigarette and gave Alice a careful little touch on the arm. I was always careful when I touched her lately, like if I touched her too hard she would just break into pieces.

"How're you doing today, Al?"

She glanced over at me quick, nodded, and she reached down and took a big drag of that cigarette like she wanted me to notice what she was doing. Maybe it was a cry for help, I don't know. I took it like that anyway.

"When'd you start doing that anyway?" I said, pointing at the cigarette as if she didn't know what I was talking about.

She shrugged and then smothered it into the aluminum foil. I waved my hand in the air to push the smoke away. I never liked smoking, me. Got disgusted by the smell of it. For a moment, I wished I'd found Alice out on her tire swing in the back yard because some fresh air woulda been good right about then. I could see why she wasn't out there all that often any more, though. Being out there, watching on her girls, probably made her think too much of Grace, and how Grace wasn't playing in the field with her sisters. Alice reached over to her right side and pulled out a pack of cigarettes, which was half full, and took another one out. Menthol, they were. Funny. I had a friend who smoked those things when she had colds because she said it cleared her sinuses. Alice stuck it in her mouth and offered me one, but I shook my head. She shrugged again and lit her cigarette, taking another long tug at it before placing it back on her ashtray.

"You know, that ain't good for your girls," I said, and what I said surprised me, because I never butted into anything Alice did in the way of parenting. But I couldn't help it. That smoke, it got into everything. It danced up to the ceiling and then spread every which way, for sure into the girls' room, and that meant they were sucking it in too.

"They're fine," Alice said.

"Why don't you let me take 'em out back for a bit? Play around and all that."

"No, thanks."

"We won't go anywhere, Al, we'll just stick around the field."

"No!" she said, and that was the first time she ever snapped at me.

Right about then I dropped any talk about her smoking. I thought about the paper airplanes I saw on the ground outside the girls' room, and remembered how their bedroom window was open, so that made me feel a bit better about it anyway. The smoke'd just find its way out into the air and maybe wouldn't bother the girls too much. That was about all I could take of sitting there with Alice, though, and it sounded like she had about enough of me, too. It was a different kind of talk than we usually had, but it wasn't better either. It was weird for me because I always loved being around her, even if we was sitting there together all quiet, but what I really wanted to do was see the girls. So I let out a big sigh and pulled myself up from the couch.

"I'm gonna go check on the girls," I said, and started to walk out of the living room when she stopped me for a second.

"Hey, Gideon," she said.

"What's that?" I said.

"You ever think about getting out of this place?"

"Like outta the rez?"

"Yeah, like out of the rez, out of *here*."

"Well, I don't know, I guess so, sometimes," I said, and the truth was I did think of it from time to time, but not seriously. I wasn't about to leave Alice and the girls, or my grandpa neither, especially since he hadn't been feeling too good lately. I didn't think I could stand living away from any of them.

"I've been thinking about that," she said, and she wasn't dragging on her cigarette then. She wasn't staring at the TV set neither. She was looking out the window, out into the sky hovering over the big field her girls used to always play in. "I've been thinking about maybe heading out to the city."

"Alice, what would you ever do in the city? Your home's here and all your family ... and me, too, you know."

"That's just it, everything I know is here, and I don't want to know all that anymore," she said, and that's when it started to make sense to me, because if the memories in the house were crushing the girls, they were crushing Alice too.

"You know," I said, "my grandpa always says you can't run away from memories and emotions and shit. They're faster than you could ever be."

"Fuck what your *grandpa* says," she said.

That was like a punch in the stomach to me. I just stood there like I was frozen or something, until she finally took another drag of her cigarette.

"Anyway, that's what I've been thinking," she said, like she hadn't just swore at me.

"Okay, Al," I said.

I turned away and went off to the girls' bedroom, not really knowing what else I could say to her, or if I wanted to say anything at all.

When I walked into Kathy and Jayne's room, I found the two of them going about their own business, almost oblivious to each other. That wasn't a natural thing, to me, because they usually did almost everything together. It wasn't like playing in the field, of course, but it was still together, you know. Jayne had a box of crayons spread out on the floor in front of her, along with a stack of paper, same kind of paper I saw outside the bedroom window on the ground. She was in the middle of scribbling letters on one of those pieces of paper in red crayon, and she was real into it. I could see her little pink tongue sticking out of her mouth she was concentrating so hard, like Michael Jordan when he was driving to the hoop. I smiled at that. That was real cute to me.

Kathy, she was sitting by the bookshelf with her legs curled right up into her chest, her eyes stuck into a novel that looked kinda big for a little girl to be reading. She was holding it up to catch some light coming in from the bedroom window. The girls didn't notice me when I came in. They didn't look up or nothing, which was odd, because, like I said, they really loved me lately.

"Hey, Kathy," I said as I stepped deeper into the room.

At that, she looked up and smiled quick, but only quick, because right away she was looking back at her book. The closer I got, the more I could notice about the book she was reading. It looked like one of Alice's.

"What're you reading? Anything good?"

She looked up again, this time to shoot me more of an annoyed look rather than a smile. Then, like she didn't know what she was reading, she turned the book over to look at the cover, and flipped it back around.

"*The Lovely Bones*," she said.

"That sounds kinda awful," I said, and that's really all I could say about it, because I didn't read much, and I never heard of that book before. Hell, you could probably list off 20 book titles to me and I'd be lucky to know one of 'em. Kathy, she'd probably read more books than me and she was just 10 years old.

"It's about a girl who gets *killed*, Uncle Gideon, and then she becomes a ghost and helps solve her own *murder*."

"Well at least she gets to be a ghost and all," I said. "That's kinda nice."

"I guess so, but she's *kinda* stuck in purgatory. So, I don't think it's all that good."

I walked over and sat down beside her, cross-legged, and, without asking, I took the book away from her and began to look it over more carefully. I could read and all, in case you're wondering, I just didn't think it was too exciting as an activity. Rather be doing other things I suppose.

"Maybe I'll read it," I said. "Maybe you should be reading, you know, the books you got in here."

She snatched the book from me real fast, before I could even think of grabbing onto it tighter. Jayne didn't even notice any of what Kathy and I were doing; by that time she'd finished writing whatever she was writing, and now she was folding that same paper up with just as much concentration, her tongue sticking out and all. It looked like a little stick of gum, like at any moment she would blow out a breath and it'd turn into a bubble. Kathy looked at the bookshelf and rolled her eyes.

"Uncle Gideon, these are *kids* books, they're little *baby* books."

"Well, that's what you are, aren't you? You're a kid, Kathy."

"Plus, I've *read* them all, and I don't like reading the same thing twice. It's boring."

"I just don't think you should be reading something sad like that, that's all. Don't seem right to me."

"Well, you aren't my *dad*."

"Damn right I'm not your dad," I blurted out without thinking.

Right away I could see that what I said hurt Kathy, probably just as much as what she said had hurt me. Those girls still loved their old man, despite what he did to Alice. Kids just love their dads I guess, and there ain't nothing you can do to stop that love, even if the person who's getting the love don't deserve it—and that bastard sure didn't deserve getting loved by Kathy and Jayne. Still, it wasn't for me to say who the girls loved, and, as soon as I said what I said, I felt bad about it. When they got older, they could decide for themselves about him. For now, I figured I needed to keep my damn mouth shut.

"God, I'm sorry about that, Kathy," I said, and I reached over and gave her shoulder a squeeze.

Kathy put her book down and put her head on my shoulder for a moment, then took it away and buried her eyes back in her book. I gave her a little tap on the shoulder, and when she looked up again I motioned over to Jayne.

"What's your sister up to?" I whispered so as not to disturb Jayne; I didn't want to break her concentration. By that time, I could see the paper she'd been writing on and folding up had turned into a crude airplane. So, that mystery got solved, even though I wasn't sure what she woulda been writing on those airplanes. If you didn't know any better, you'd think Jayne was just any other normal five-year-old girl. I mean to say, you'd never guess by looking at her what she'd been through in her life. She didn't look altogether sad, unless you looked real deep into her eyes, and she was done up just like I liked to see her, like a girl her age liked to dress. She was wearing one of her dress-up princess gowns, Cinderella I think, and she was wearing it as nice as a real princess. Better, even.

"Oh, she's making *arrow*-planes."

"*Aira*-planes!" Jayne snapped, suddenly joining the conversation.

"Oh, right," Kathy said with a snicker.

"What're you building those for?" I said to Jayne.

Jayne got up with the paper airplane in her hand and looked it over with a whole bunch of pride. Then, with a smile kind of filled with wonder, she pinched the bottom of the plane between her thumb and pointer finger and started flying it around the room, even making airplane sounds here and there, the typical kid sounds for machines and such. You know, it coulda been the sound of a tractor for all I knew, but it was nice to see her make-believe. And I liked that she was flying the plane around the room, too, because it felt a bit like she was dancing and twirling like she used to. Even her feet were up on their chubby little toes. Those toes were so cute, you just wanted to play this little piggy with 'em.

"I jus' felt like makin' aira-planes," she said as she flew her clumsy contraption.

I thought about the big pile of them outside the window and wondered why she was throwing them away, because she seemed to like them a lot just to get rid of 'em. I don't know, maybe she was trying to make the perfect one and she hadn't quite made it yet. They were all, like, prototypes or whatever. I figured if she eventually made the perfect one I could pick up the others when I left so they didn't litter the whole rez. Lord knows, there was enough junk layin' around here and there, mostly in the ditches between the highway and our houses. Like old broken tricycles or blown-up car tires or Tim Horton's coffee cups or other shit like that.

"Yeah, but what're you *doing* with them, Jayne?" I said.

She stopped spinning and held it out in front of me like it was a treasure she found. I think I let out an "oooh" and an "ahhh" to make her happy.

"*Ooooh* ... she's doing something real smart with them, I can tell you that much," Kathy said in a real snotty tone.

"Shut up, Kathy, you don' even know," Jayne said.

"Sure I do. You're writing little notes down on them and chucking them away," Kathy said, all matter-of-fact.

"Well, *yeah*, but that's not what I'm *doing* with 'em!"

"What in the heck else could you be doing then? Littering, that's all!" Kathy said.

"I'm not littering!" Jayne shouted, and she started to cry real hard, and the airplane dropped to the ground like a leaf falling in autumn, rocking back and forth like Alice's tire swing out back. Jayne dropped to her knees and buried her head deep into her lap, and her body started to sob in time with her crying. That just about broke my heart. Truth was, I'd never seen her cry yet, not since Grace died. I think it took Kathy by surprise too, because just as soon as she was tellin' Jayne off, she was over beside her little sister, her arms wrapped all the way around her. I went over to Jayne too, me, and I took them both into my arms. We ended up like one of them Russian nesting dolls, and just like we were connected, after Kathy started to cry, I found there were a few tears running down my cheek, too. And just like Jayne, well, I'd never cried yet neither. We stayed like that for a few minutes until arm by arm we let go of each other. We ended up sitting cross-legged in front of each other in a crude little circle, and the airplane Jayne made was in the middle.

"I'm not littering," Jayne said again, this time with a bit of a quivering lip.

"Okay, Jayne," Kathy said.

"What're you doing with them, honey?" I said.

She picked up the paper airplane again and moved it around in the air without getting up, in slow motion. She didn't use sound effects either. I guess she was thinking about why she was making them in the first place. Sometimes kids did things without thinking about it much. Like, on impulse. You know: something seems like a good idea, and that's that.

"I jus' wanted ta do something nice, I guess," she eventually said, without taking her eyes off the airplane.

Well, I wasn't sure what she meant by that neither, because, according to Kathy, all she was doing was chucking them out the window after she played with them. I was careful not to challenge her, of course, because Kathy had pretty much traumatized her a few moments earlier. So I said, real careful, "What do you mean by doin' something nice?"

"My mommy use-ta tell me this story about a sad princess that lived on a cloud, all alone and away from the world, an' one day there was a prince who was real lonely too. He knew about the princess, cuz everybody knows about princesses in clouds, you know that?"

"Everybody knows that," I said.

"So, ummm, he went an' wroted *notes* to her. An' because he couldn't fly, he tied the notes to a bird's leg, an' got the bird to fly them to her."

"What kinds of things did he write about, now?"

"Just nice stuff," she said, "like what I'm writin'."

I asked her, after that, what kind of stuff *she* was writing, but Jayne, she wasn't havin' none of that. She said telling me about what she wrote in those paper airplanes would've been just like telling somebody about a wish you made, and if you did that, well, your wish wasn't ever going to come true. She couldn't stand thinking about somebody not getting what they needed from those notes of hers, so she told us it was a secret she wasn't ever going to spill. "And then I go like this," she said, and she ran over to the window and threw it as hard as she could out into the air.

"Where do the notes go?" I said.

"Doesn't matter," she said, and walked back over to her paper and crayons, spread another piece out onto the floor, and began scribbling some more words down in red crayon. "They jus' go up and up and fly to whoever needs 'em."

"That's real nice, Jayne," I said, and I looked down at her with the same kind of wonder she looked at her airplane with. She was a real treasure, that one.

"You can make one," she said without looking up at me, too intent on writing her words, and I was sure not to peek at what she was writing, too, because I didn't want to spoil none of the magic she thought she was making.

"Okay," I said.

I took one of the pieces of paper, picked up a crayon, a "royal blue" one, and began to write down my own words, ones that would make the saddest princess I could think of not so sad anymore. When I was done, I folded it up into the nicest paper airplane I was able to make. I looked up to wait and see when Jayne was finished hers, and that's when I saw Kathy was making an airplane too. It didn't take them long to get them ready. When they were, we all walked over to the window. I lifted up the curtain and we all counted to three together. On "three," Kathy and Jayne let theirs fly. Kathy's almost flew all the way to the other end of the driveway. Jayne's, well, it went where I figured it'd go. Jayne noticed I didn't throw mine, and she got real annoyed at me.

"Hey! What're you doin' Uncle Gideon? You didn't throw your aira-plane!"

I knelt down beside her and looked her right in the eyes.

"Jayne, I'm going to take this airplane to the highest place I can find, and throw it way up in the air so it gets to the very saddest princess. Okay?"

She thought about this for a long time. Finally, she nodded all sweet to me, fell back down on her knees, and started to make another plane. Me, I had other plans, so I began to walk out of the room. Before I left, Kathy ran up to me and gave me a big squeeze around the waist. That felt real good, and I turned around and squeezed her right back. I squeezed her so hard she let out a big *ooomph*. When I let her go, she walked back over to the bookshelf, sat on the floor, and tucked her legs into her chest. She picked her book up and started to read it again.

"Bye, Uncle Gideon," both those girls said without looking up or waving.

"See ya, girls," I said, and left them to their things, their books and airplanes.

I walked back out into the living room and saw Alice still sitting there. She was sucking back one of her menthol cigarettes, watching another talk show. I wished something for her, but I ain't going to tell you what I wished. If I did, you know, it wouldn't ever come true.

"I'll see ya tomorrow, Al," I said, and she gave me a nod.

I stepped outside and ran my hand along the trailer as I walked back up the driveway. Stopped at the girls' bedroom window. I bent over, picked up all the paper airplanes, and stuffed them down my shirt so they wouldn't fall out or blow away. Before leaving, I held out the airplane I made. I pinched the bottom of it between my thumb and pointer finger, cocked it back real far, and tossed it through the window, into the girls' bedroom. Then I kept on walking: I navigated around Alice's barricade, got into my car, and started driving down the highway. I ended up driving all the way around the rez that day, and without any real destination. As I drove, every once in a while I threw a paper airplane out the window. It didn't matter where they landed, neither. They just went up and up and flew to whoever needed them.

FIVE

Terrence didn't have a cause to be at the cemetery, didn't have any close relatives or friends buried there. They would've all been buried at his own rez, which was a couple of hours west. But he went to the cemetery from time to time because he thought people didn't visit the dead often enough. So, every once in a while he found somebody to visit.

The first time he visited Grace, it was before winter, but the weather had already begun to turn. As he walked through the cemetery, he listened to the sounds hiding within the silence, how blades of grass beneath his feet crunched like gravel, how leaves that hadn't fallen yet gently rattled in the breeze. He walked past headstone after headstone, all unique, just like faces in a crowd, all imperfect, cracked, and weathered. He thought about the headstones, how people spoke to them through tears and rested flowers upon their crests like crowns. He thought that cemeteries were like stone beauty pageants.

He was compelled to stop at Grace's burial site at first because he loved the headstone; it was shaped like an opened book, and he hadn't seen one like that before. He was used to crosses or cherubs or upright ones that were square or oval shaped. Then he looked closer. On one side of the book, the moon's soft white light rested upon Grace's neatly etched name, and the years she'd been alive: 2011-2014. So young when she died—hardly enough time to know the world and what it held for her, or for the world to know her. He hated seeing children's graves. What had she been like? He always had the same question for the dead. He made up stories for them.

Grace, she was a cute one, with thin black hair and a button nose, and, at three, a handful. But chasing her around was a joy. She got so wound up that she needed to have a story read to her before bedtime or else she couldn't sleep. Love You Forever. *Terrence had been read that story as a child. It was a good one for Grace. On the other side of the headstone he read the name* Alice. *There was no date of death. Her mother. Alice, she missed her baby. She read stories to an empty bed because she missed her so much.*

Terrence wiped a tear from his cheek. He would come visit Grace again. He'd bring a book and read to her.

STARFISH

"HEY."

Alice couldn't believe her ears. It was Ryan.

She sat speechless for a long time, long enough that she thought—perhaps hoped—he would hang up. Why now? Why hadn't he called after Grace's death? She had a sense of what the answers might be from hearing Ryan's fractured and weak voice. The tone was out of character for him. It had always been either loud and aggressive, or minutes (sometimes hours) later, it was honeyed and apologetic. *Manipulative* might be the best word. He would call her a slut or a bitch, depending on what he was mad at, hit her a few times, or more, go for a walk, then come back and talk sweet to her, tell her how much he loved her, tell her that he'd never do it again. Then, the next day, or the next week, he'd lay hands on her again, scream at her, then cool off and be in love with her. One day, on one of the longer walks he took, she remembered going to the bathroom door and telling the girls it was safe to come out. When the door opened, she saw how their bodies were trembling, how pale they looked, and their eyes were wide and wet with tears. That's when she'd called the RCMP.

It was for them, not for her.

And still she had no words for him as she sat on the couch with the phone to her ear, listening to him breathe. He'd been locked up for over a year now, and during that time he'd called her twice, both times before Grace had been killed, and both times she'd hung up on him before he could finish saying hello. Yet now, though she hoped he would hang up on her, she couldn't hang up on him. Not this time. His voice stopped her. She worried, despite herself, that it would break him more if she dismissed him again. She hated that she felt that way. She greeted him back, then, with words as hollow as she could muster, words with no intonation, and so without emotion. He didn't deserve emotion from her.

"Hello, Ryan."

"How're you holding up, Alice?" he said.

"I'm doing how I'm doing," she said.

"I, uh, I loved Grace. I hope you know that. I'm dying over here," he said.

"Well you would've been *here* if you hadn't done what you did. It's nobody's fault but yours."

"I know," he said.

"Grace," she said before stopping to hold back tears, then continued, saying, "she could've used a father. To protect her, you know. She isn't ever going to know who you are." Another pause, then, "Or what you did to me, to the girls."

"I didn't do nothing to those girls and you know it. I love them."

"I know you love them, but don't think for one second that you didn't do anything to them. And you should've been here for her, for all of them."

He didn't say anything. She could hear him breathing, hear men in the background shouting at him to get off the phone. She wanted to hang up then, even took the receiver away from her ear and let her thumb hang over the end button, but then replaced the phone to her ear and took a calming breath. There were things she needed to know, now that he was on the phone with her.

"You know every time you beat on me, those girls were locked up in the bathroom after you left. I found them there each time."

"I know. You told me they were in there."

"But do you know who put them in there? Did you ever see anything?"

"Anything like what? I thought they'd just gone in there on their own."

Her heart sank, although there was no reason why he would've seen anything. He was too busy concentrating on her to notice anything else. That's what she'd been trying to do lately, though—trying any way she could think of to confirm that the girls had really seen angel. She would stand in the bathroom for hours on end waiting for the angel to come; pace up and down the hallway, looking over her shoulder to see if it was behind her; lie down on the spot where Grace's body was found and look up at the stars and wait to see something, anything; and she even found herself praying about it. She'd lie in Grace's bed, cuddle up to one of her stuffed dolls, and talk to God, ask why, ask Him to show her a sign so she would know Grace was okay. God never said anything back to her, not a whisper, not a gust of wind through the window to move the curtain just so. In the end, Alice knew kids found ways to cope with bad things and there probably never was an angel. If there was, why hadn't it saved Grace? But she wanted there to be an angel. If there was an angel then there was heaven, and if there was heaven then surely Grace was there.

She heard more shouting in the background, louder shouting. It reminded her of him, the tone she was familiar with.

"Look, I gotta go," he said. Then he paused and added, "I'm sorry Alice. I really am. For Grace. For everything, you know."

And there was that sweet voice again, the tone she knew all too well, the tone that had tricked her time and time again.

"Don't call here again," she said.

She hung up the phone, then calmly walked outside into the cold.

There was Alice, on her tire swing at the back of her house, staring out across the untouched field of snow, which looked—with its subtle drifts and undulations—like an ocean frozen in time. As late as it was, she could see just fine. The winter sky was a soft orange, and it painted the barren scenery in front of her as an overhead streetlight would in the city. But she saw nothing she wanted to. She had no jacket, but it wasn't because the cold didn't bother her—her body was shivering more and more with each passing moment, her skin cool and hard. It was because she didn't care. Perhaps she cared too much about other things. She was crying, and those tears had formed into tiny patches of ice across her cheeks. Every time she blinked, her eyelids would try to freeze shut, and she would struggle to open them again.

Eventually she heard the sound of crunching but gave no notice. The sound drew closer and closer until it was right beside her, then it stopped altogether. She felt a light touch on her shoulder—against her deadened skin it felt like getting touched on an area frozen by local anaesthetic—but she didn't turn around. She knew it was Gideon; he was the only person who came and stood beside her as she sat on the tire swing. They were beyond the need for greetings. They remained in silence for a long while, until she could hear the swishing sound of glove against jacket as he tried to warm himself, and his teeth chattering uncontrollably like a set of wind-up dentures. Despite this, he didn't leave, and she didn't acknowledge him. It became something of a battle of wills. Alice tried to endure his presence long enough that he would give up and she could be alone and stare out across the snow in peace.

"What're you lookin' at, Al?" he finally said.

She knew he didn't expect to hear anything back from her. She'd been this way lately every time he came by. He'd been persistent at first, made every attempt to try to talk with her, keep her company. Eventually, though, he'd stopped trying. This had relieved her, because, as much as it hurt her to hurt him, she didn't want to talk to anybody about anything. She just wanted to be sad and angry. So, he'd begun just saying hi and then heading over to the girls' bedroom, where he played games with them, or read stories, or did pretty much whatever it was they were doing at the time. She knew he was doing that. She heard him and the girls laughing and having fun and appreciated it, although she never told him that. She knew somebody had to spend time with Kathy and Jayne. She couldn't bring herself to do it.

"There's nothing out there, y'know," he said.

He breathed out, his breath rose up then dissipated. Alice responded, saying blankly, "I know, I just wish there was."

"What do you wish was there?"

This was met with no response.

"It's getting real cold, Al. We should get inside."

Alice knew she wasn't going to have a choice in the matter. Gideon was never going to let her stay out there in the cold. He'd given up on talking to her when coming over to visit, sure, but this was different. He looked about ready to pick her up and carry her inside, and she knew he would've, too. She took one last look out across the great white nothingness and reluctantly, slowly, got up from the tire swing, causing the rubber tire to push away and rock back and forth, the first time it had moved at all. She turned away from the field and made her way to the trailer with Gideon following close behind.

Once inside, Alice walked directly over to the couch and sat down, replacing stares into the snowy field with stares into a blank television screen. She was shivering, and her skin was pale. Gideon went to fetch a comforter and placed it snug around her body. He sat down beside her and gingerly put an arm around her, trying to give her some of his warmth. Alice didn't move through all of this, just kept staring at the television screen. Perhaps to make things less weird, Gideon eventually reached over and turned the television on. Of course, she didn't watch the television, didn't even notice what channel it was on (it was, not surprisingly, on a children's station). Instead, as she stared at nothing, he stared at her, perhaps wondering what was going through her mind. Eventually, some time in the night, after Alice had fallen asleep slumped over with her head resting on the side of the couch, he left her side.

The next morning, Alice woke up on the couch alone, and, to her surprise, didn't like the feeling. She never would've admitted it to Gideon, but she had liked having him there with her last night. She was sure that he'd saved her. There wasn't any way she was going to tell him this, however. She wasn't ready to. She didn't need to seem vulnerable. She hated the thought of pity, the thought of people looking at her with sad eyes, thinking how bad they felt for her but how lucky they were that what happened to her hadn't happened to them. Gideon never treated her like that yet, but if she got soft around him he surely would, and then she wouldn't want him around. It was odd; she wanted to be alone but hated to be lonely. As her eyes adjusted to the light, and her mind adjusted to wakefulness, she heard voices from the kitchen table: the laughter of her girls and Gideon's voice telling jokes. She was glad to hear him and wondered if he'd left at all.

"Look," she heard Gideon say, "your mommy's awake, how about that?"

Alice sat up on the couch and looked over to the kitchen table. Her daughters waved. She waved back.

"Morning, Mommy!" Kathy and Jayne said in unison.

"Good morning, darlings," she said.

Gideon met eyes with Alice and pushed a small bowl of cereal across the table in her direction, an offering for her. She shook her head but thanked him. She ate when she had to, but never felt like it, and it usually wasn't until noon that she ended up putting some food into her mouth: crackers and cheese or a few chips. Gideon shrugged and pulled the bowl back toward him, then sat down and started eating the cereal.

"More for me," he said. "Gonna get soggy otherwise. Right, girls?"

They nodded. Alice did, however, get up from the couch and join them at the table, and this was a rare occurrence, and in some ways more surprising than if she'd taken a bite of cereal. She pushed some hair away from her face and took a sip of Gideon's coffee. He offered her the whole cup, so she continued to sip it as she watched her girls eat. She used to enjoy that, watching them busily eat their breakfasts, scraping every last bit into their mouths, hearing them chew with their mouths open. She never much cared to teach them table manners, always thought it was more important for them to just be kids. But watching them now, as much as she loved them, didn't give her the same amount of joy, because her eyes would always trail over to where Grace used to sit, and she would be reminded of how there was one less mouth chewing. And Grace, well, she was the most fun to watch eating. Half of the food would get on her face, shirt, or table, and she'd play this game where she dropped her utensil and made one of the girls pick it up for her. They always did, too. Nobody sat in her chair. Nobody could anyway; Alice had never taken the booster seat off.

"Hey, Al," Gideon said, "I told the girls maybe they could play in the snow out back after breakfast. Whaddya think?"

Alice shook her head. "No, I don't want them playing back there today, Gideon."

The girls let out a collective, disappointed sigh. Gideon did too. It was strange to Alice, before and after Grace died, to see such a rough-looking man acting so often like a little girl, but he played with them at their level whatever they were doing. He was one of them, and they loved that about him.

"Come on, Al, they're cooped up, these girls. They're goin' stir crazy is what they're goin'. How about just for a little bit?"

"Gideon," Alice pleaded.

Letting the girls go outside gave her anxiety. She didn't like the thought of them being anywhere they could get hurt, and so them being inside was about the safest place they could be. As one month bled into the next, she had let them go outside less and less, and, when they were outside, she was out there with them.

"Please, Mommy!" the girls said.

Alice turned to Gideon with a disapproving look and whispered, "Not really giving me much of a choice, are you, asking right in front of them."

"Grandpa used to…," Gideon started but was interrupted quicker than lightning with a stern *don't* from Alice. He raised both his hands in surrender.

"Just sayin'," he said.

"I guess you can go," she said to the girls, then to Gideon added, "I'm coming too."

The girls shrieked happily and ran off to their bedroom to get changed. Kathy even left her plate out on the kitchen table, which she never did. It had been well over a week since they stepped out the front door of Alice's trailer, other than when they had to use the outhouse.

"Great," Gideon said. "Make sure you wear a jacket this time, though."

"Fuck off," she said.

It wasn't long before the four of them were out behind Alice's trailer. The girls were trudging through the field's deep snow with great difficulty and, it should be said, great joy, and Alice and Gideon were at the tire swing. Alice was sitting in it and Gideon was standing at her side. It was a touch milder than last night, but only a touch. Alice could see that Gideon was already cold; his shoulders were hunched up to try and keep warm and he was dancing around in one spot like he had to pee.

"You know, next time you're in the city, you should get a damn parka. You've had that windbreaker for years," Alice said, at which Gideon nodded, perhaps too cold to say anything.

The girls were warm. They were bundled up in thick snowsuits, unable to move their limbs very much, navigating the deep snow with stiff arms and legs. They looked like starfish might look, if starfish could walk. Gideon chuckled every now and then at their awkward movements. Even Alice did.

After they were out there for a little while, the two girls fell flat on their backs for no apparent reason. Out where they were, the snow had drifted so high that the two of them nearly disappeared from sight. They didn't get up, either. Alice and Gideon looked at each other, sharing confusion, and were curious enough that they moved from their spots to get a closer look. They walked slowly so as not to disturb the girls. As they drew nearer, it was still hard to make out what the girls were doing, both of them flat on their backs and just below the surface in an untouched area of snow. It looked as though they were in convulsions; wafts of snow were kicking up into the air as though from tiny snow blowers as their arms and legs moved rapidly back and forth. They were laughing so uncontrollably they could hardly breathe.

When Alice and Gideon got right up to the girls, they saw that they'd been making perfectly shaped snow angels. Gideon laughed at the sight. He gave Alice a touch on the arm as though she hadn't noticed. Alice wasn't laughing, but all the same, she was enamoured with the girls' creations. She stared at the angels with the same look as when she'd been staring out into the orange-tinged field last night.

"He's here," Alice said breathlessly.

"Who's here?" Gideon said.

"He's right here."

She fell backwards. The sensation reminded her of being on the tire swing after she'd gone as high as she could—that moment before coming down to the earth. There was a freedom to it; how her stomach dropped, how her heart began to race, and, most of all, the weightlessness. When her body sank into the snow, it felt as though she were submerging herself in water, the flakes so deep and thick and soft. It felt as though she had never landed, that she never would land. She looked up to the sky, a perfect blue, and began to desperately move her arms and legs up and down and side to side. Her eyes welled up with tears that quickly froze against her skin. She didn't stop for a long time.

SIX

There'd been another baby before Kathy was born. Back then, Alice's mother was still alive but suffering badly from diabetes. Her mother was sad all the time. She knew what was happening to her and that she didn't have much time left. But when Alice told her about the baby the sadness went away. She took Alice into the city and they shopped for baby things together—clothes, a high chair, toys. During that trip, her mother didn't seem all that sick.

Then, one night, Alice felt cramps in her belly, and when she turned on the lights, she saw blood between her legs. Olive rushed her to the hospital in Innis, but to Alice there was no need for the hurry. She knew what had happened. And as crushed as she felt, because she'd always wanted a baby, she felt worse for her mother. The sadness would be worse than ever.

A few months later, Alice got pregnant again. She spent the first three months praying like she'd never prayed before, even though she wasn't sure anybody was listening, and was nervous right up until Kathy was born. Kathy got all the things that Alice and her mother had bought for the unborn baby. By that time, Alice's mother had lost her legs and was fading fast at a hospital in the city. Alice didn't want to bring Kathy on a trip to the city when she was so young, so Alice had Olive bring her mother a picture of Kathy. Days after the picture's arrival, her mother passed away. Olive said that the picture had been placed at her mother's bedside and she'd stared at it for hours on end.

SWEET TOOTH

NEVER BEEN IN JAIL BEFORE, ME. Never really been in trouble about anything, except getting in shit from my grandpa and all that, when I was younger. But, you know, your grandpa ain't gonna throw you in jail. So there's a difference there, too. And people always say good things about me. I mean, people don't go around talking about me all the time, but I think, mostly, folks around here would tell you that ol' Gideon wasn't any sort of a troublemaker. Anyway, the fact of the matter is that my sweet tooth got me thrown in jail, and that's screwed up if you don't know the whole story. I shoulda damn well known better, and that's that. Call it a, whaddya say, cautionary tale, I guess.

It was just heading into spring and most of the snow was gone. There were spots here and there of the stuff where it drifted the highest over the winter, but most of it had melted and made its way into the lake. Everybody was worried about flooding, of course. Every spring it flooded around where we lived. Anyway, I was at home picking over a microwave TV dinner. Hungry Man's meal, they call it. One of my favourites, you know. That's about when I started to have a pretty bad craving. See, just a few hours before that, I'd been at Alice's house spending time with Kathy, Jayne, and ... shit ... almost always say Grace, me. Getting better at that, though. Not forgetting her, mind you, just remembering that she isn't around anymore. So, I was with the girls in their bedroom playing tea party. I don't really care what you think about that neither. I'd pretty much do anything for those girls. If they wanna play tea party, then Uncle Gideon's gonna play tea party.

We did that for most of the afternoon. "Course, we didn't have real tea or anything like that. We drank out of pretend tea-cups that were really Dixie cups filled with sterilized lake water, ate pretend cupcakes that were really ripped up pieces of stale bannock, and pretend liquorice that was really red pipe cleaners. Got all dressed up, too. Yeah, the girls got all done up in princess dresses and good ol' Uncle Gideon went and snuck one of the only dresses Alice had and put it on. Like I said: anything for those girls. That afternoon was different, though. It got difficult for me; it was one of those times that Grace's absence seemed bigger than normal. Wasn't any good reason for it, neither. I just noticed her bed, which was still made up perfect like it always was; her stuffed animals huddled up around her pillow; and her empty spot at the tea table. She used to play with us when she was around, but now Jayne and Kathy put her favourite stuffy there, a big Dora the Explorer thing. After all that playing, Alice asked me to stay for supper, but I told her I didn't feel like eating anything, which was true. I really didn't. My stomach felt all in knots and sore.

I ended up going home, and that's how I got to picking at that Hungry Man dinner. Like I said, that's my favourite thing to eat almost, besides Alice's bacon and eggs. But I wouldn't've felt like eating that neither if she'd offered it to me. Guess I wasn't much of a hungry man right then. What I did feel like eating was some real treats, not fake cupcakes or fake liquorice. I wanted to eat treats real bad. Problem was, diabetes kinda runs in my family. I don't have it yet, but I still gotta watch what I eat pretty close. I'd always been pretty good about that, too—I hadn't ate junk in a long time. Still, there I was getting that craving, for liquorice and a bag of peanut M&Ms to be exact. I knew it wasn't a good idea, of course. But, before I knew it, I was putting on my boots, my windbreaker, and heading out the door on my way to the grocery store.

The grocery store was pretty close to my place, and I decided to walk it rather than take my truck. I figured that, on account of the round trip, about four miles altogether, I'd get enough exercise that the junk I was planning to buy wasn't gonna bother me much. I was, like, bargaining with myself about it. To give myself an even better excuse to go and buy that stuff, I thought I'd get something for Kathy and Jayne, too, while I was at it. You know, since Grace died, the girls hadn't been given much of anything. I thought they'd really like some jujubes or something like that. I'd even pick out the yellow and the black ones for them, because nobody liked those ones anyway.

Most of the walk over to the grocery store was a stroll through a bunch of nothing after nothing, especially if you'd walked that way thousands of times like me. If there was something to see, though, it wouldn't have mattered anyways, because all I could think about was the liquorice and peanut M&Ms. After about 15 minutes I got to the centre of the rez. "Downtown," as I like to call it. I walked by the Adult Ed building, by the Elders' home, and, finally, made my way by the community hall, which was a stone's throw from the mall and doubled as the gaming centre. I never spent much time over there at the hall. Never played bingo, which was mostly what went on there, and I was never much of a gambler neither, so never had a reason to go into the gaming centre. Yeah, I wouldn't've given that place a second thought, woulda been happy to pass by it and be even closer to the mall, because the grocery store was in the mall, and my liquorice and peanut M&Ms was in the grocery store. So, you could just imagine how annoyed I was when I heard an old familiar voice call at me.

"*Hey*-uh, Gideon," said the voice. It sounded almost exactly like Baby Huey from those old cartoons.

I stopped right there in my tracks, closed my eyes, and cursed. I didn't turn around at first, kinda wished I was imagining that I heard what I did. But pretty soon there were big, heavy footsteps coming toward me, then little bits of gravel sliding as feet skidded to a stop right behind me. I turned around and came face to face with Gunner, a big-chested, bigheaded, pencil-legged piece of work I'd sworn off as a friend over a decade ago. Tell you the truth, I was surprised he stopped me at all because we hadn't spoken for God knows how long. I usually avoided being around anyplace he was at. Whenever I saw that stupid Sunfire of his, I just turned and went the other way. I didn't see it anywhere in the parking lot this time, though, so he got one over on me there.

"Hey," he said, "what've you been up to?"

"Nothin' much," I said.

"Oh, yeah?" he said.

"That's what I said isn't it?" I said.

"*Geeeeez-us*," he said, taking a long time to spit out the word, like he was trying to sound as offended as possible.

I turned away, started walking toward the mall. I hoped he wouldn't follow me. Stupid me. He didn't take the hint, followed me right when I started to walk away, caught up to me quick, and started walking with me step for step like we were soldiers.

"You comin' from the health centre?" he said.

I didn't answer.

"Man, I got one chick over there at the health centre, Roxie. You know her?"

I stuck my hands into my windbreaker, kept walking in my own silence.

"She's a chubby little bitch, but man she can screw. I'm screwing her all the time, just got to call her. She's my booty call."

"I'm not coming from there," I said.

When I got inside the mall, I passed by the lottery booth and made a beeline for the grocery store, sharp and quick, like I could lose him or something. Shoulda known by then that he wasn't goin' nowhere though, for whatever the hell reason. He was like one of them damn rez dogs begging for food. Probably woulda rolled over if I asked him to. I stopped right in front of the grocery store, and he stopped beside me.

"Yeah? Where're you coming from then? Alice's place? You two are close aren't you? What's she like these days?" he said.

"She's fine," I said.

I looked out across the store and tried to recall what aisle I needed. I generally ignored the junk aisle, like I said before, but it wasn't that hard to figure it out, because there was only four aisles in total. Aisle two was the one I wanted. I walked down that way, passed by soda pop, chips, and then got to the candy and chocolate bars. Bunch of vitamin water around that way too, all in rows one over top the other, and all different colours. Shit, all those bottles looked just like a rainbow. Anyway, that's where I landed up, and that's where Gunner followed me to, picking up and opening a bag of ketchup chips on the way.

"Aren't you and Alice screwing or something? I swear I heard you're screwing," he said in a muffled voice, his mouth full of chips.

"What the hell are you talkin' about? God, you're a real shit," I said.

"*Shee-it*, just curious," Gunner said.

There we both were, standing in the aisle surrounded by a bunch of junk. All I wanted to do was grab my stuff and go, but he was standing in my way, between me and the cash register. I woulda went the other way, to the back of the store and then all the way around, but I didn't think he deserved that much of an effort from me. So I didn't go, on principle alone.

"What do you *want*, Gunner?" I said.

"Say, you ever think about that little girl? What's her name, that *little* girl … uhhh…," he said.

"Grace," I said.

"Yeah, Grace. You ever think about her?"

I picked up a pack of peanut M&Ms and rolled it around in my hand.

"I do, yeah," I said. "Always do. Think about what she might've become, all that."

Gunner shrugged, like he didn't care to hear the answer even though he'd asked the question. I reached over and picked up a package of liquorice to go with my peanut M&Ms. I got to thinking about how I was saving money by getting junk for supper. That'd always been funny to me, how a big bag of candy was cheaper than fruits or vegetables. Yeah, I coulda bought a few bags of candy for the same price as a carton of milk. Stupid.

"Yeah," Gunner said. "But, you know, she *could've* been a real nobody too, if she'd gotten the chance to be anything. She *could've* been a real shit. Kids grow up that way from time to time."

Well, I don't know what else to tell you about that. I dropped the liquorice and the peanut M&Ms faster than you can say go, and then I grabbed Gunner by his stupid Metallica T-shirt with my left hand, and punched him straight across the jaw. Felt that thing bust into pieces. Heard it crack, too. It sounded just like when you crack your knuckles all at one time, you know. He flew against the candy display and a whole bunch of candy bags came showering down over his head like rain; M&Ms, Reese's Pieces, Nibs, Clodhoppers, and every other candy you could think of. I stared at him there for a moment, along with a bunch of other people who'd come running when they heard the commotion. We were all standing there staring at him. He was out cold. His head was resting to the side and there was this sound coming from his mouth that was kind of like snoring but kind of like gargling water. If he wasn't lying in a heap of candy, and there wasn't blood dripping from the corner of his mouth, you woulda thought he was having a nap.

Me, you woulda thought I'd just run a marathon. I'd only just decked the bastard but I was sweatin' like crazy. My hand hurt like a bitch, too. Anyway, it wasn't long before Randy, the manager, showed up.

"What happened over here?" he said.

I didn't answer him, just stood there rubbing my hand, kinda worried I broke the damn thing, to be honest. I'd never punched anybody before in my entire life, and, with how I was feelin' right then, with the sweating and the pain in my hand, I was sure I wasn't going to do it again.

"You'd better get out of here, Gideon," he said.

"Yeah," I said, "that's a pretty good idea."

I got home about 20 minutes later. I took off my boots and my windbreaker, went to get a bag of frozen peas for my knuckles, and got all settled in. Ended up laying down on the futon with my head against the armrest. I flipped through channels on the television until I found a good crime show, a *Law and Order* spin-off. SVU I think, not that it matters. Not long after that, my eyes kind of trailed down to the microwave dinner I'd heated up for myself earlier in the evening, and wouldn't you know, I felt like eating. I reached over and picked up the tray and rested the food right there on my stomach. Now it was as cold as one of them piles of snow out around the rez, but I didn't care about that. With my left hand—the one without the ice pack on it—I picked up a chunk of "steak" and shoved it in my mouth. I say "steak" because that's what it was *supposed* to be, and it was the only kind of steak I really ever got to eat, but it was more like a hockey puck or something like that. It tasted pretty good. Coulda used some ketchup, mind you, but I ain't ever been picky. I must've been pretty tired, though, because I fell asleep before I could take another bite.

When I woke up in the morning, there was an infomercial playing about some kitchen tool in place of the crime show I'd been watching, and that bag of peas had gone and melted on me, right across my pants, too. I got up to throw my food in the garbage, and when I looked down I saw that it looked like I'd pissed myself. I went over to my dresser in the corner of the room, pulled off the wet pair of jeans, and fished for something else to wear. Ended up finding an old ripped pair that I had. I got one leg into them when I heard a knock on the door. I didn't have any clock around me that worked, so didn't know exactly what time it was, but it felt pretty early for somebody to come see me. Hell, nobody ever came to see me no matter what time it was anyway. I was usually the one who went and saw people.

I hopped across the room to the front door, walking while trying to get my pants on. Opened the door while zipping them up. I guess I shouldn't have been surprised to see Ernie there with his cop getup on. Even had the cop car behind him still running. He looked pretty serious; his mouth was stuck in a frown, and it made his wrinkles seem deeper and longer. I ain't ever seen Ernie like that, actually. He was usually hiding behind the desk at the RCMP detachment in the rez, playing some kind of game on the computer. He was always happy, too. Point is, I was surprised to see him at my door, whether I should've been or not. Guess I thought nothing would happen after I punched Gunner out. Or at least I never thought too much about it. Honestly, people get punched out around here all the time and I'm not sure how many of 'em get in trouble for it. Then again, most folks don't get punched in the middle of a grocery store in front of a bunch of shoppers and workers and shit. So, it was what it was.

"Hey, Gideon," Ernie said.

"What's up?" I said, even though I knew exactly what was up.

"I heard what happened last night," he said.

"I guess *so*," I said.

"What were you thinking?" he said.

"I was thinking he was being an asshole," I said.

"There're lots of assholes out there, Gideon. You can't just go punching them all."

I didn't put up much of an argument when Ernie said he had to take me in. I knew I had to go. So, I put my windbreaker on and got in the car. I wanted to walk over to the detachment, it wasn't very far, and I felt like fresh air would've been good considering I was about to get locked up, but Ernie wouldn't let me. He did let me ride shotgun though. That was good. I woulda felt like a real criminal sitting in the back seat.

Before too long I was sitting in my cell, and I have to tell you, sitting inside and seeing it from the outside are two different things. You know, I'd been in the detachment before, but I'd never been there on account of something I'd done. It might sound like a bit of a cliché, but there wasn't much to do in there but sit and think. I got to thinking in a roundabout way, though, because at first all I was doing was looking across the room out of boredom. It had three white walls and one wall made of metal bars. It was small in there, but that didn't bother me too much. My house was small, too. There was a bed but no pillows or sheets. Guess they didn't want people gettin' too comfortable. Out on the other side, the free side, there wasn't much to see, neither. There was a desk that Ernie was sitting in, the reception desk, I guess, and then a couple more desks in the room where the other cops sat. Other than that, there was just a bunch of posters on the wall. One of them caught my eye, though: a recruitment poster for one of those Aboriginal programs that tried getting people jobs. There was this good-lookin' Aboriginal woman in a police uniform smiling big and wide on it. I'd been to a few of those programs in the past. Anyway, when I looked at that poster, I started to think about what Gunner said when he went and got himself punched out. You know, about what Grace woulda been if she didn't get killed. She coulda been a police officer for sure. She was feisty, that one— little but fierce. Hell, she coulda been anything she wanted to be.

Thinking about Grace got me thinking about Alice and the girls, and thinking about them made me feel pretty lonely even though I hadn't been in there for too long. I figured I could ask Ernie to use my phone call. I knew I got one of them from all the crime shows I'd watched. From the way I was feeling, I thought the best thing woulda been to get them to come over and visit with me, maybe at the same time get Kathy to bring me over a book, something like that book I seen her reading a long time ago. *The Lovely Bones,* I think it was. I didn't read much, me, but I woulda read right then, and a sad book like that woulda been a good one for me. Course, that wasn't ever going to happen; Alice never left her house any more, and she certainly wasn't gonna leave to come visit me in jail. It woulda been good to talk to them, though, whether they came or not. You know, hear a familiar voice.

I was about to ask Ernie about that phone call, too, when I saw the front door open. I went and hid in the corner faster than you could imagine. It wasn't that I was scared or nothing, you know, but I sure was embarrassed. Like I said before, I knew most people around the rez, and nobody thought I was one to make any trouble, and I didn't want people to think that now. I listened real close as heavy footsteps made their way across the room and then stopped. I didn't know many people who had footsteps like that. Started to wonder who it could be. Even when the person started to talk, I had trouble placing the voice. It was real low, and all the words kind of jumbled together. Sounded kind of like they were talking without their lips open.

"I'm not supposed to allow that," I heard Ernie say.

After that, I heard footsteps coming in my direction. That was a surprise to me. Couldn't think of who would come to see me. Hell, nobody even knew I was there. I woulda thought that maybe Ernie called Alice to come by, like he'd had the same thought as me about needing some company, but Alice didn't walk like that and she didn't sound like that neither. As the footsteps approached my cell I looked for somewhere else I could hide, but of course there was nowhere I could go. Woulda looked like a real idiot slipping underneath the bed, seeing as how it stuck right out from the wall like one of those floating shelves. I ended up walking out from the corner and sitting down on the bed just as the footsteps stopped. I was looking away at first, maybe because I was too ashamed to look up, in case it was somebody I knew real well, but I figured I had to eventually, so I did.

Gunner. Of all the people, it was Gunner standing at the bars beside Ernie. I got all warm in the chest and I wasn't sure if I was angry or I felt bad for the bastard. Might've been a bit of both, I guess. His jaw was all swollen up, and the left side of his face was pretty much blood red. When I saw that, I got why he was talking funny. Musta been hard to say anything with his face looking the way it did.

Ernie set down a chair and motioned for Gunner to sit, which he did.

"Hey-uh, Gideon," Gunner said.

I looked at Ernie.

"What's going on?" I said.

"Gunner's come by to talk to you," Ernie said, all calm.

I didn't get why he sounded like that. Me, I was pretty far from calm. My chest just kept getting hotter and hotter, and my right hand started to hurt again like it was trying to remind me about what I'd done. I kept trying to think of why Gunner would be coming to see me after I'd knocked him out, but I drew a blank.

"I don't really think I want to talk to him, Ernie," I said.

If he was there for anything, I thought he was probably going to bark at me for getting caught like I did, throw it in my face. I didn't need nobody to do that to me. I was doing that fine on my own.

"I think you should hear him out," Ernie said.

"Do I have a choice?" I said.

"Not really," he said.

Gunner and I shared an awkward look.

"You gonna bark at me or something?" I said.

Gunner shook his head.

"Fine, I guess," I said to Ernie.

Ernie looked us both over, as though he wasn't really sure if he should be leaving us like he was, even though we were separated by the bars and all, but then he took a deep breath and walked away.

"I'll give you two some privacy," he said as he settled back at his desk.

I tried my best not to look at Gunner, but I couldn't keep myself from stealing glances at him. It's like when you see a car accident, a bad one, and you don't want to stare but you do anyway. That's a good way to put it, I guess, because Gunner's face sure looked like a car wreck or something. His jaw was crooked and because of that his whole face looked bent this way and that. Whatever he'd come there to talk to me about must've been hard to say, too, because there was a whole lot of silence right then. I couldn't stand that. I wanted him to say what he had to say and leave. In the end, I figured if I said something, he might say something back.

"Look," I said, "I'm sorry about hitting you and all. You were being a shit, and I got mad but I shouldn't've hit you."

Gunner leaned forward in his chair. He tried to rest his face against his hand, but I guess he forgot about his injury. He winced and sat up straight.

"I'm not mad at you, you know," he said. "Not really."

He didn't say anything for a little while, and I didn't say anything neither, because I wasn't sure what I woulda said in the first place. I'd already said everything I wanted to say, me. Not much else I could do but apologize. So, while I waited for him to keep talking, I killed time counting the metal bars. I got up to 13 before his lips opened a crack, probably about as far as he could manage.

"Everybody does things they wish they wouldn't have done," he said. "I guess that's what I'm trying to say."

"Okay," I said. "Thanks."

"I might've punched me, too, you know. If I was you," he said, and he said that real quiet, like he didn't want me to hear. But it felt good to hear it, and I figured that Ernie was right about letting Gunner talk to me.

"I'm glad you come to see me," I said.

"Yeah?" he said.

"Yeah," I said. "I been feeling pretty heavy about it this morning but I feel a bit lighter now."

Gunner rubbed his hands against his knees. And he was doing it hard, too, because I could see his knuckles get white.

"We've both been feeling heavy about things I guess," he said. "We both regret things."

"What've you got to regret?" I said.

He didn't answer me. Instead, he stood up like he was about to leave. I stood up too and put both my hands against the bars. It felt kinda weird to me right then, because at first I didn't want him to be there, and now I didn't want him to leave. Imagine that, me wanting Gunner around. It'd been years since I could say something like that. He started to turn away.

"Gunner," I said.

He turned back to me, put his hands in his pockets, but wouldn't look at me.

"I'm sorry about Grace," he said. He opened his mouth a crack, closed it, and then opened it again. "What I said about her. I'm sorry."

"Yeah, sure," I said.

He gave me one last little head nod with that big ol' head of his—kinda looked like a bobble head, him—and then turned around and left me standing there. Walked right out the door after I seen him nodding to Ernie. I didn't know what that was all about until a few minutes later, when I was sitting on the bed again, and Ernie come up to me and unlocked the jail cell. He swung the door open and motioned for me to step outside. You woulda thought right then that I'd jump up and run out of there, but I didn't even get up. I couldn't wrap my head around what was happening.

"What're you doing?" I said.

"Gunner doesn't want you to be in here. He asked if I'd let you out, forget everything that happened."

Ernie stepped to the side to give me a clear pathway. I stood up, took a step or two forward but didn't leave then neither.

"You sure you heard him right?" I said.

Ernie shook his head. "He's talking funny because of his jaw, but there was no mistaking what he said."

"Gunner said that he didn't want me in here?" I said.

"What do you think, that I'm playing a prank on you? He was real clear about it, okay? Now, I could keep you in here if I wanted to, but honestly I don't want to and neither does ol' Randy at the store. Now stop looking all funny at me and get the hell out of there."

I don't think I'll ever understand that one, but eventually I did step outta that jail cell. Ernie offered me a ride home, but since I was a free man at that point I told him I'd rather walk. It wasn't a long way from the RCMP detachment to my house anyway. When I got outside, the air felt fresh to me, and I took a few deep breaths before starting on my way. I guess you could say I was smellin' freedom. And right then it didn't matter that I'd walked around there a thousand times, because it felt like everything was new. Even the way I was feelin' was new. You know, for years I'd thought that Gunner was a big piece of shit and that's that, especially after what he'd said to me about Grace, but I don't think I felt like that any more. I mean, I didn't like what he said, I never would, but then he'd gone and done that kindness to me. I'm still not sure why he went and did that, but maybe all I have to know is that he ain't all that bad.

Anyway, I didn't even end up going home. I landed up heading over to the grocery store. "The scene of the crime" is what they'd say in one of my crime shows. I wanted to get some candies for Kathy and Jayne, you know. Ended up getting them some of those jujubes, without the yellow and black ones, of course. I didn't get anything for me, though. By that time my craving was all gone.

SEVEN

Jill stood with Amanda in the foyer of the reserve's school as their children scuttled off to class. The school was only about three years old and looked just about as nice as any she'd seen in the city. Better even. Jill and her friend were both staring at the new addition to the foyer, a set of large wooden carvings that represented the seven sacred teachings. There was an eagle, a buffalo, a bear, a beaver, a turtle, and a wolf. Jill counted them, and then counted them over again. She scratched her head.

"They're missing one," she said.

Amanda counted the carvings carefully, pointing at each as she did.

"Hey, you're right," Amanda said.

"They have six, and there're supposed to be seven," Jill said.

"Yeah, I know. I can count," Amanda said.

They looked at the carvings carefully, each of them trying to figure out which one was missing.

"Mistapew is missing," Jill said.

"Oh, yeah," Amanda said.

"That one's going to look deadly when it's finished," Jill said.

At that moment, a girl about the age of six tugged at Jill's pant leg. Neither woman had noticed the girl standing there.

"Did ya know that Mistapew's a really good hider?" she said. Jill nodded.

"They say that's why nobody can ever find him," the girl said.

Jill smiled, and so did Amanda. Then the girl pointed out the front door, where in the distance the forest was visible.

"You see those trees over there?" the girl said.

"Yes," Jill said.

"They're trees, all right," Amanda said.

"It could be right there and ya'd never know it," the girl said.

The girl walked away without another word and left the women staring into the forest.

SIMPLE MOMENTUM

As a sixteen-year-old girl, Sara wasn't typically quiet. Neither was her mother, for that matter. Yet there they were, sitting at the dinner table, picking at their dinner and not saying a word. Their chewing and the tick of the cuckoo clock that hung over the stove were the only real sounds. And every once in a while they would hear water slapping against the sandbags at the back side of the house—it was almost up to their back door at this point—but they'd become so accustomed to it that the gentle clap, clap, clap didn't register. Sara wondered, as she picked at her food, if other houses in the area were just as quiet as theirs, if the people within them were all forced to listen to chewing and ticking and clapping. She couldn't imagine it any other way. It had been a tough time for everybody.

Earlier in the year, her little cousin Grace had been killed, and Auntie Alice had been getting sadder and sadder. It was so bad that they never really saw her any more, and, when Auntie Alice was seen, she was out on her swing in the back yard, even during the coldest days of what had been an abnormally bitter and snowy winter. Due to all the snow, when spring came, the lake overflowed and the flood began. They'd been waiting the past two days for an evacuation order. Many people had already left for the city regardless, but others like Sara and her Mother decided to stay home until they absolutely had to go, because being home was way better than being in the city. Auntie Alice, well, she had either left the rez entirely or just wasn't coming out of her trailer. Sara wasn't sure.

And, as though Grace's death and the flooding wasn't enough, young women on the rez were committing suicide. By now there'd been five deaths, one after the other. Each time one girl died, it seemed to get easier for the next. It had become a trend, like wearing yoga pants or UGGs or cowboy shirts. Sara had started searching the Internet for "suicide by hanging" after her first friend had been found dangling from the soccer goal outside the school. One girl, Margaret, hadn't been successful. (Sara learned, via Google, that 70 percent of people get it right—meaning, they die one way or another.) She was at the hospital in the city now, brain damaged. It seemed like all the girls were doing it, "stringing themselves up," the teenagers called it. The fifth and most recent death, just yesterday, had hit the hardest. Angela, one of Sara's best friends, had been found hanged by her belt from a coat rack in the motel at the side of the highway. Sara couldn't help thinking about what Angela would've experienced. She would've got scared as she began to lose consciousness. She would've grabbed at her neck. Panicked. After learning about Angela, Sara had locked herself in her bedroom. That would've scared the shit out of her mother if she hadn't been able to hear Sara crying nonstop. When Sara did come out, her mother saw that she'd smashed up her laptop. It was in pieces on the bedroom floor. Sara didn't want to learn about suicide any more.

"You know," Sara's mother finally said, "the Elders say there're bad spirits around here causing all these things to happen. They say they're stuck in the air, moving from one place to another, infecting everything just like a cold."

Sara rolled her eyes. "And the Christians think it's the devil," she said.

Her mother shrugged. "Well, it's the devil or it's bad spirits, one thing or the other. Maybe it's the same thing anyway."

"Well, at least they're agreeing on something," Sara said.

Her mother ignored her and said, "What we need is a big cleansing, that's what we need."

"If only the rez was flooded with holy water," Sara said.

"Don't be a smartass," her mother said.

Sara picked up her fork and shovelled a forkful of macaroni into her mouth.

"I know two of those girls were close with you, and it's hard to lose friends," her mother said.

Sara shook her head and stabbed at a single piece of macaroni. Then, under her breath, she said, "They weren't that close."

Sara wanted her mother to stop talking about it. She wanted the silence back. But her mother continued anyway, saying, "You have little girls like Grace dying before they even get a chance to live, and then your friends are choosing to die. I know it's a waste, and I know it's hard to understand."

"Yeah," Sara said, "but there's no point making stuff up just to feel better about it. Spirits and demons. People just make things up when they don't get what's going on."

"I don't think that's true at all," her mother said.

"And you know what else? Gideon's grandpa, he used to tell me about Bigfoot, too," Sara said. "This whole place needs to learn that there isn't such thing as Santa Claus."

"Sara, lots of people around here believe in Mistapew," her mother said. "And we need something like that around here right now, even just the belief in it."

Sara rolled her eyes. Her mother ignored this too.

"Be true to yourself. That's all Mistapew means. Honesty, Sara. That's a teaching," her mother said.

"Yeah, a teaching, not an actual thing," Sara said.

"You know, old Victor down the road took a video of the thing a couple of years ago," her mother said.

"He took a video, Mother, of somebody in a Chewbacca suit," Sara said. "You know, like how people put on red suits and white beards."

Her mother took tiny bites of her dinner. It didn't seem like she was putting much into her mouth, more just doing something to do something. She said, "Maybe you should've gone to some of that counselling at school. They've got good people over there, you know. They could help you."

"No," Sara said, "they couldn't."

"Well, you're just impossible then, aren't you? Impossible."

"I just don't want to talk about it. Can't you see that I don't want to talk about it?" Sara said.

"You have to talk about it to somebody," her mother said.

But Sara was done talking to anybody, especially her mother. She thought none of it mattered anyway. Bad things lead to bad things, and they didn't need the devil or some bad spirits to help. It was just simple momentum. Her mother reached across the table to touch Sara's hand, but Sara instantly pulled her hand away and took to finishing her supper as quickly as she could. When she was done, she disappeared into her bedroom, shutting the door behind her.

Her mother finished eating her dinner in the same quiet that had covered both of them, thoughtfully chewing each forkful and looking at Sara's empty chair as though she was still sitting in it. When she finished, in the silence, in the soft din of ticking clocks and the sound of clapping water against the back of the house, she whispered a prayer. Later, she would go to her daughter's bedroom door and place her ear against the wood. She would listen for her daughter's voice, for her daughter's feet moving along the floor, for any sound that would set her mind at ease. Then, she would open the door a crack and walk down the hallway to her own bedroom. She would lie down in her bed and stare at the ceiling, resigned to believe in the prayers she had offered.

Deep into the night, Sara was woken up by gentle knocks against her bedroom window. Facing the wall, she rolled over 180 degrees to read the alarm clock, and groaned when she saw the time: 1:07 AM. In the hazy state between sleep and wakefulness, she ignored the sound at first. She'd been dead asleep and wanted to remain that way. She hadn't slept the night before, after Angela died, and now her body, and her mind, had given out on her. So she ignored the knocking, hoping it had been a dream. However, as soon she lay her head back on the pillow and closed her eyes, the sound came again: a light, almost apologetic, knock. With a frustrated sigh Sara kicked off her comforters, got out of bed, and went over to the window. She climbed up onto her dresser and peeked out to the front yard, where she saw Flora, her best friend, who sheepishly waved. She hadn't seen Flora since Angela had killed herself. Sara slid open her bedroom window and stuck her head out into the cool midnight air.

"What are you doing?" she said.

Flora didn't answer, although not for lack of trying. She opened and closed her mouth several times. A few times she stuttered the beginning of a word but stopped. Finally, she threw her arms out to her sides and let them fall back against her thighs with a light slap, like the floodwaters gently clapping against the sandbags out back.

"Are you okay?" Sara said.

This was followed by a short period of time where the two best friends simply stared at each other. This was an odd silence. Flora and Sara were never at a lack for words. They usually talked all through school (including all through class, which got them into trouble on a near daily basis), they texted all through the day, talked on the phone almost every evening, and in all of those interactions there was never any quiet. They talked about boys and school and movies and life and even about nothing—trivial things—but never *nothing*. Sara saw Flora, in the careful light of the overhead moon, as she had never seen her before. That light, like television static in the dark, glinted off Flora's usually vibrant eyes. They looked tired and lost and desperate all at once. Finally, Sara motioned her friend forward. Flora took Sara's outstretched hand, scaled up to the bedroom window with her help, and climbed inside.

They got down from the dresser and stood in the middle of Sara's bedroom, two feet apart, Sara looking at Flora and Flora looking to the floor. Sara wasn't sure what to say or do, so eventually she took Flora's hand and guided her to her bed, and they both lay down together, face to face, curled up together, their bodies clumsily forming the shape of a heart if viewed from overhead. Sara had Flora's hands in her left hand, and with her right hand stroked Flora's raven black hair away from her face. Still, Flora said nothing, but rather looked into the pillow as though there were something to see there, something which begged for attention.

"What can I do?" Sara whispered, at which Flora shook her head lightly, and, even though each strand of hair was pushed away from her face, Sara continued to run her fingers through Flora's hair. Then, in the dim light that occupied the bedroom, Sara could see a tear fall from Flora's eye, followed by another, then more, and as more tears came, dampening the pillow, her body began to shake. She pulled her knees into her chest and hugged them tightly with both arms until she was curled up into a ball. Sara found herself shushing Flora as she would a child, as she used to do with Grace when her cousin was just a baby, when her crying was uncontrollable, with hiccup breaths and a heaving chest.

"It's okay, I'm here," Sara said. "Everything's going to be fine."

"But it isn't," she said through tiny huffs of breath.

"Let me get you a Kleenex," Sara said and tried to get up from the bed, but Flora reached over and held her down. Sara relaxed back beside her friend and gathered her deep into her arms so her head was pressed between Sara's neck and shoulder.

"There's a curse here, there is, there is," Flora whispered into the nape of Sara's neck.

Sara thought this wasn't the time to tell her that there was no such thing as curses. She simply shook her head and squeezed Flora tighter. But she became angry at the whole idea of there being a curse. Not because Flora thought it, but because she could be made to believe such a ridiculous thing by others. There was a curse. There was the devil. There were bad spirits. People were trying to find reason in the unreasonable. Girls were killing themselves and it needed to make sense somehow. Now there was Flora, buried deep in Sara's arms, so close against her body that the two were almost one person, suffering together, talking about curses, which more than likely made Flora all the more distraught.

"I want to die," Flora said. "I just want to die. I can't take it any more. Everybody's leaving me."

"They're not leaving you, they're just leaving," Sara said.

"I do want to die," Flora whispered as she began to play with a tiny strand of her own hair. Strange, Sara thought. If she kills herself, her hair will keep growing, like it doesn't agree with her decision.

"No, you can't," Sara said.

With each word she held Flora even harder, pushed her friend deeper and deeper into her embrace as though to hide her from the darkness.

"You can't leave," Sara said. "You can't leave me."

Everything Flora was going through, Sara was going through, had gone through, yesterday and today, and each time a friend of theirs died. Sara didn't think she would ever take her own life, but how much loss could one person endure? She couldn't stand to think of it. She pulled Flora closer, closer. She clasped her hands behind Flora's back. She couldn't leave now, not if she tried. She would hold Flora there forever if she had to. She would never let go. But eventually, against her will, Sara's mind began to drift into the darkness she was trying so desperately to keep Flora from.

She blinked out a tear, another, then her eyes remained shut as she fell asleep.

With Flora still in her arms, Sara awoke to the sound of footsteps methodically making their way across her bedroom. She didn't open her eyes at first. She was sure it was her mother coming to check on her and didn't want to deal with the questions. What is Flora doing here? And, if Sara answered that honestly, she would have to talk about spirits and demons again, and she wanted no part of that. So she decided to pretend to sleep until the footsteps retreated, back outside her bedroom door. The footsteps stopped at the side of her bed. Sara did her best impression of sleeping. She kept her eyes closed for at least a minute but in the end felt it far too disconcerting to picture her mother standing over her and Flora, watching them. So, she opened her eyes.

Sleep brought haziness to everything: her thoughts, her sight. The first thing she saw was black, even though she knew she was facing the window. She should've seen moonlight coming in from outside. Her curtains weren't drawn, and her mother wasn't big enough to blot everything out. She began to search the room without moving her head, shifting her eyes this way and that way. There was light against the wall by her head, against the wall near her feet. There was light, just not in front of her. It was as though a big black cloud had seeped in through the window and settled in her room, right beside her bed. She rubbed her eyes. Things became clearer. Her eyes began to adjust to the darkness. The shadow sharpened. It reached almost to the ceiling. It was fuzzy, too. And the fuzziness wasn't due to her waking eyes. No, Sara realized that the shadow, the figure, was covered in hair. That's when her other senses began to drift in: the smell of wet dog, the sound of heavy, deep breathing, the sensation of that breath coating her body like a blanket. She begged for it to be a nightmare, as awake as she felt. She pinched herself aggressively on her hip.

Nothing made the thing disappear; it seemed only to grow larger and louder.

She knew it then, what stood before her. She knew it as the beast bent down and removed her arms from around Flora's body. Its touch sent a cool shiver that started at Sara's arm and spread throughout her entire body, like a morphine drip. "Mistapew," she said breathlessly as it placed its arms underneath Flora's body and effortlessly lifted her up. It turned around and walked out of the bedroom. Sara got up and followed it through the house. Both the hallway and the kitchen were eerily silent, devoid of the usual sounds of clocks ticking and faucets dripping and the house set-tling, the conversations of the night. It was as though she and Flora and the great beast were frozen in time, or removed from it. The only sounds were their footsteps, but even those were whispered to her ears. She was led to the back door, where they stopped.

"Where are you taking her?" Sara said.

It looked back at her, a quick glance, then turned to the door, opened it, and stepped outside. Sara started to as well but stopped when the cold waters tickled her foot. She didn't remember the waters being so high, or so cold. She had only a nightgown on. The beast continued walking with Flora, farther away from Sara. A small wake gathered behind them that looked like a pathway in the moon's light. Against her better judgement, she took a deep breath and stepped outside, submerging her feet into the water. Her body tensed, and goose bumps rushed across her skin. She clutched her arms at her sides in a vain attempt to retain some body heat. She could feel mud push its way between her toes with each step, and the ground felt like a wet sponge beneath her feet.

"Flora!" she called out, but there was no response. Flora was asleep, limp in the beast's arms as it brought her deeper and deeper out.

"Where are you taking her, please?" Sara said. "I thought you were supposed to be honest!"

She followed for as long as she could, until the water reached up over her chest, pooled around her neck, and touched her chin. And, even then, she was prepared to swim if it came to that, ready to follow Flora and the beast for as long as she could. But the thing stopped about 10 feet away, with the water only up to its waist, in an area of calm, a place that stretched endlessly toward the horizon. And the water was black all around because the stars were shy that night, except for the reflection of the moon overhead, which touched the water near where they stood, the soft but generous white glow rippling like a flag in a delicate breeze. There, in the stillness, Sara watched as the creature turned Flora's face toward its own. It breathed gently across her cheeks, which caused her eyes to flutter, then open.

"Flora, are you okay?" Sara said.

Flora didn't answer, but as she stared at the great beast she didn't scream, didn't start, didn't try to get away. She simply lay there nestled in the creature's arms, the rising of its chest rocking her back and forth as a cradle would a baby. She looked as calm as the water that surrounded them. This brought peace to Sara as well, and she called to her friend no longer.

She saw Flora try to close her eyes, to fall back asleep, but the beast placed its hand against her cheek and shook its head. "No sleep," it said in a deep voice that rumbled through the air and across the water, causing tiny tremors. Flora nodded. It turned her over and lowered her close to the water.

"Look," it said.

She did.

"Do you see?" it said.

"I'm beautiful," Flora whispered.

Then the beast submerged its hand under the reflection of the moon, and the white light pooled into its massive palm. When it brought its hand up, it brought the light also, so the water beneath Flora was now black, her reflection gone along with the moon's.

"Drink," it said.

She placed her mouth at the side of its hand and allowed the water to spill over her lips, down her throat. When she was done, her head went limp against the beast's arm. She was asleep once more. The beast turned toward Sara and began to walk back to the house, Flora tucked safely in its arms. Sara walked with them, following them when it entered the house, through the kitchen, down the hallway, and back into her bedroom. She started for her dresser in order to rummage through it and find some dry clothes to put on, but, for the first time, she noticed her nightgown was dry.

Is this a dream? She kept patting at her clothes to find wet spots, but there were none. And yet she felt awake. Everything felt real. How is this possible?

"Are you here?" she said to the beast, but it just stood there, silent, waiting.

Sara lay down, and the beast placed Flora beside her, and she took her friend back into her arms. Without a word, it walked out of the bedroom and left the two friends behind. It's real. It was real. Sara drifted back to sleep thinking these words as she stared out the window, deep into the sky, where the shy stars lay hidden, where the moon and its generous light seemed dimmer. And she could only reason, as her eyelids grew heavier, that some of the light was now in Flora.

Sara would wake the next day and find that she and Flora talked the way they used to talk, and in those words there was no room for silence. Her mother would make pancakes with scrambled eggs, which was a rare treat, and Sara could only guess that her mother was happy to find her brighter, just as Sara was happy to find Flora brighter. Flora would leave after breakfast, and Sara would stand in the doorway and wave goodbye. Flora would wave back and smile and her smile would be returned. And all of this is not to say unpleasant things had not happened, because surely they had, and all of this is not to say there weren't still unpleasant things to come, because surely there were. But, if there were bad spirits there were good ones, and if there were demons there most certainly were angels. Sara would think about this as she considered the new things she had learned and what she had seen. And the following night she would pray the good spirits would visit her auntie, wherever she was, because brightness caused brightness. It was simple momentum.

EIGHT

After returning home from the hospital, the first thing Alice did was go to her bedroom. She closed the door and put Grace down on the mattress so the moonlight coming in from the bedroom window fell across her three-day-old body. Alice listened, but the trailer's usual sounds were absent, replaced instead by the soft cooing from Grace's tiny mouth. Olive had taken Kathy and Jayne over to her place, and Ryan had stayed in the city with some friends. She'd been upset at first that he would even think to do something like that, leave her and their newborn girl alone, but it wasn't long before she welcomed the idea. It was peaceful.

Alice stroked Grace's cheeks and lay down beside her. She watched as her baby's eyes darted around as though looking at everything, but she knew Grace could only really focus on her mother's face. Alice liked that. Grace's arms and legs were twitching involuntarily. One day they'd move, bring her to the most amazing places. But, for now, she was right where she needed to be.

STARING AT THE SUN

S HE THINKS OF THE PAST, all those yesterdays. She wants them back. No tomorrows. She dreams asleep, she dreams awake. The dreams are nightmares, even the pretty ones. The pretty ones are the worst.

Alice reaches for the remote, her distraction. She flicks the television on. It's Dora. Alice imagines Grace, her baby, is in front of the television set, telling the characters where to go. She touches the glass with her dirty fingers. She gets smudge marks everywhere. She always gets smudge marks everywhere. When Alice wants to watch her shows at night, everything seems out of focus from the fucking smudge marks. But Grace isn't really there. Alice flips through channels, settles on a daytime talk show. Midday bullshit. The picture is crisp and clear. No dirty fingers. No dirty glass. She would do anything to have to use Windex.

She lies down on her side, pushes a pillow underneath her head, and curls her legs into her stomach. She sticks the remote between the pillow and the couch. Her baby is crawling on top of her, bending down so her face is obstructing Alice's view of the television set. She wants attention. The more annoyed Alice gets, the harder Grace laughs. She tosses her baby to the other side of the couch. Grace laughs, what a fun ride. She crawls back over to Alice, crawls up to her shoulder, lowers her head. "Stop it!' Alice says. Grace laughs. She crawls all over Alice's body like goose bumps. But Grace isn't really there. Alice wishes for the weight against her shoulder. She wants her baby to annoy her, wants to shout at her. She wants goose bumps.

She falls asleep and dreams she is listening to Grace breathe, listening to her talk, savouring words like a delicacy. Her voice is sharp, sifting effortlessly through stagnant air, through the aroma of stale cigarettes. Alice moves with the sound, along the air, through the window, into the cool morning breeze. She looks at Grace from the outside, her baby's eyes melting into her cheeks with that smile. Then she blends into the breeze and is gone. When Alice wakes up, she thinks, for a moment, she is back beside Grace. Her tiny breaths like warm kisses, her tiny cheeks squished against the couch, a trail of saliva drizzling from her lips, her tiny feet pressed between Alice's thighs. But her baby isn't really there. Alice's breaths are her own. Her face is cold and lonely.

Alice makes breakfast for Kathy and Jayne in the morning. They pile out of their bedroom, sleepy, their feet dragging along the floor, their hair dancing every which way like flames, their eyes adjusting to the light. She makes two more plates than the ones she prepares for Kathy and Jayne. She always makes two extra plates. One of the plates almost always gets eaten while the other does not. But Gideon isn't there this morning. That means he's either sandbagging for some extra cash or with his grandpa at Innis General Hospital. She doesn't blame him, of course, but the girls look sad in his absence. He makes faces out of the bacon and eggs—the over-easy eggs are eyes, the bacon is a mouth. The girls laugh so much at that. So, one plate lies uneaten in front of Alice. She won't eat it. The other plate is in front of Grace's booster seat. Alice imagines her there. She picks up the bacon like a lollipop. It's more a toy than food. She licks it, chews it, bangs it on the plate like she's drumming, just like she used to see her daddy do. She eats around the yolk. She hates the yolk. Sometimes, she'll sneak it onto Kathy or Jayne's plate. They'll eat it. But Grace isn't there. The bacon and eggs will get cold, jealously untouched.

Alice watches Kathy and Jayne eat. They are tidy about it. They are quiet, too. It wasn't always this way. They used to eat like hungry rez dogs. She wonders if they see Grace too, like she does. Alice will send them back to their room after breakfast. She wonders if her baby will be there, if she'll play tea with them, or run around bugging them as Kathy tries to read and Jayne tries to colour. Of course she will. She always does. But Grace isn't there.

She looks around the room—the kitchen, the living room. She thinks about the hallways. It leads to the girls' bedroom, her bedroom, and the bathroom. There is nowhere else to go. The trailer is small, so small that her baby can be everywhere. The walls hold memories inside like cigarette smoke. She looks at the booster seat, the uneaten plate. She runs out of the kitchen, down the hallway, into her bedroom. She is gasping for breath. The tears blur her vision like the memories.

She rushes to the corner of her bedroom, rummages through a pile of dirty clothing until she finds two black duffle bags, one of them emptied, one of them full. She unzips the full bag. Dirty men's clothing—tube socks, tighty whities, jeans, T-shirts, a hooded sweatshirt. Ryan's stuff. She rummages through the bag, pulls out a faded red Spider-Man T-shirt. She holds it out to inspect it—the ink stain on the left shoulder, the hole along the right side. She used to like that she could see his skin through it. She scrunches it up and holds it against her nose, breathes violently. Clean laundry. He always smelled, always smells, like clean laundry. No matter what he did or where he went, always.

She changes into the T-shirt. It's loose and makes her look ragged, but she doesn't care. She zips the duffle bag up and slides it flush against the corner of the room, piles dirty clothes back onto it, either to hide it or protect it in her absence. She takes the other empty bag and fills it with clothing; hers, Jayne's, and Kathy's. The girls' clothes smell like Ryan. They are like him in that way. Grace, too. Alice packs just enough clothing to get by. There's always Walmart in the city. It's cheap there. Big and crowded but cheap.

She calls Olive for a ride.

"Where to?" Olive asks.

"To the city," Alice says.

"Why are you going to the city? You haven't even been out of your house in forever," Olive says.

"Will you take me there, please? I can't be here anymore," Alice says.

There is a silence. Alice wonders who else would take her. She doesn't want to ask Gideon. He'll ask too many questions, and she doesn't want to talk about it, she just wants to go. He'll ask her to stay.

"I'll be over in a bit," Olive says.

"Thank you."

Alice hangs up the phone and dials her cousin, Krista, in the city. She has a big house in a bad neighbourhood. She and the girls have stayed there before.

"How long do you need to stay for? I mean, not like it matters. Shit, you can stay forever if you want. I like your kids better than mine, *ha*."

"I don't know. A while. Long enough," Alice says.

"Long enough for what?" Krista says.

"I don't know," Alice says.

"It doesn't matter anyway. Just come by whenever you can," Krista says.

Alice brings the duffle bag to the kitchen and puts it down beside the kitchen table. Jayne is finishing her food. She didn't notice Alice run out of the room. But Kathy notices everything. She looks at her mother with big, concerned eyes.

"Are you okay, Mommy?" Kathy says.

Alice nods. She looks back at her baby's booster seat. She looks away quickly, as though she'd been staring at the sun.

"But we have to go now," Alice says.

Jayne pokes her head up from her plate.

"Where are we goin'?" she says.

"Away," Alice says. "Now. Leave your plates. Just come with me."

Jayne cries out in excitement, Kathy gets up quietly. She picks up her plate to bring it to the kitchen sink. Alice shakes her head.

"I said leave it," Alice says.

Kathy puts her plate back on the table. Alice throws the duffle bag over her shoulder, takes Kathy's hand, takes Jayne's hand, and guides them out of the trailer.

Alice waits near the end of the driveway, her feet almost touching the line of rocks she made after Grace died. Her baby, she would've had so much fun on the rocks. She would've played with them in so many ways. She would've jumped over them like hurdles. She would've leap-frogged over them and got her legs caught on top of them. She would've said she was stuck and got one of her big sisters to help her down. Of course, she could've got down on her own. She knew her big sisters would do anything for her, though. She was smart.

Jayne plays basketball, throws all the different kinds of balls into the hoop and cheers each time. Kathy doesn't play. She stands by the old hockey net and stares at her mom.

After a few minutes, an old K-car pulls up alongside the highway. Olive honks the horn as though Alice hadn't seen her. Sara is in the back seat, ready to entertain the girls for the two-hour drive. She looks excited, hasn't seen the girls in a long time.

"Come on, darlings," Alice says.

Jayne bounds down the driveway, leaps over the rocks, and gets into the car almost in one motion. She bear-hugs Sara.

"You want the window seat?" Sara asks.

"Yeah!" Jayne says.

Sara swings her over to the driver-side window. Jayne laughs. Sara turns and waits for Kathy, who approaches the car methodically. She walks slowly down the driveway, steps over the rocks, and sinks into the back seat.

"Hey, Kath, I missed you," Sara says and pats Kathy on the knee.

"Me too," Kathy says distantly.

"*I* missed ya!" Jayne says.

Sara laughs. "Oh, I missed *you* too, peanut."

Alice gets into the passenger seat and positions the duffle bag firmly between her feet. Olive glances at the bag.

"How long are you planning on staying?" Olive asks.

"I'm not sure," Alice says. "A little while."

"That doesn't seem like a little-while kind of bag to me."

"It's enough."

Olive takes her hand off the gearshift and places it on Alice's shoulder.

"You sure about this?" Olive says.

Alice plays with an old luggage tag tied to the zipper of the duffle bag. She thinks of when she flew to Anchorage with Ryan. It was the only other place she'd been, other than the city. She'd left Grace to go there. She could do it again.

"Alice? Are you sure?"

Alice nods.

"Let's just go," Alice says.

Olive hesitates only a moment longer. She puts the car into drive, does a u-turn across the empty highway, and drives away from Alice's trailer. The girls are quiet then, even Jayne. The roar of the car's motor, the hum of the tires against the highway, the air whistling in through a crack in the passenger-side window, all sound deafening.

Alice sees the worried and confused faces on her girls, wonders if she's doing the right thing. But then she looks back at their home, watches as the trailer gets smaller, and her swing, and the tree, and the field. Grace is there. She is hiding in the long grass from her sisters, confounding them. She laughs, and it seems as though the grass is giggling as it flutters in the breeze. She is picking blades of grass from the ground and trying to braid them into her hair—unsuccessfully. She is bouncing up and down so in the distance it looks as though she is swimming in a lake of golden water. Alice looks away, to the highway, to the grey and the open road. She thinks of the city, where it's big and distant, and she can hide within its cold embrace.

"Where are we going, Mommy?" Jayne asks.

"Away," Alice says. "Far away."

"How far?" Jayne asks.

"Far enough," Alice says.

NINE

The boy walked outside to find his grandpa sitting on a tree stump. The old man was using a sharp knife to cut pieces away from a block of wood that was beginning to take the shape of an old shoe. There were other shoes like it around the house. They weren't like any shoes the boy had seen around the rez, though. They were fancy shoes, and they looked like people would've worn them a hundred years ago. His grandpa was beginning to work on the tongue. He'd already made little notches where the laces would go. He would use moose hide for them. The boy had seen him do that before. He sat down on the steps and watched his grandpa work, watched the strips of wood fall to the ground as soft as snowflakes. They were all in a pile at his grandpa's feet. They'd put them in the fire later and use them for kindling.

"How was your first night?" the old man said.

"Okay," the boy said.

The old man held the shoe up and blew across it. Some specs of wood flew through the air.

"You'll sleep better once you're used to it. It's always strange sleeping somewhere new, even at your grandpa's," the old man said.

There was a small pile of wood beside his grandpa that was undoubtedly going to be made into shoes as well. The boy wondered where all the shoes would go, and why his grandpa was making them in the first place. He picked up one of the blocks of wood and inspected it. He looked back and forth from his grandpa's piece of wood to his.

"Grandpa," the boy said, "why do you make all those shoes?"

The old man, for the first time, stopped whittling the wood. He placed it down at his feet and looked up at his grandson. The boy wondered if he even knew why he made them, or if he'd ever thought of it. He could relate to that. He did a bunch of things without thinking.

"You know," the old man said, "when you're born, you're like a piece of wood. As you get older and older you get carved at and carved at until you're made into something. I guess making all these shoes reminds me of that."

The boy looked down at his body and back at his grandpa with confusion. The old man laughed.

"That's what you call being figurative, Grandson," the old man said.

"Figurative?" the boy said.

"I mean, I know you're not a piece of wood, but you get cut just like I cut this piece of wood right here. You get hurt over and over again, and what you need to keep in mind is that, when those things happen, it's making you into something else. And, if you learn from all those hurts, it's something better."

The boy looked at the piece of wood he was holding, then rotated it in his hands. He couldn't imagine making a shoe out of it. What would he make, if he could? A little boat, maybe. He'd put a field mouse in it and sail it out across the lake. A short while later he went inside his grandpa's house. He walked into the kitchen, pulled out the cutlery drawer, and tried to find a nice, sharp knife.

HILROY

G IDEON PULLED UP in front of Innis General Hospital, put his truck in park, but remained in the vehicle with the engine on to ensure he had the option of leaving at a moment's notice. This had become routine recently, and each time he'd come here, he stayed in his truck a little longer than the time before. The decision to go inside or leave had become more difficult the worse things had become. It was hard to see his grandpa the way he was now, when he had been so strong for as long as Gideon had known him. Warriors like his grandpa didn't get weak. And today Gideon wasn't sure if he would end up going inside, even though, in all honesty, the threat of leaving was never that real, as much as he debated it. But the news he'd received this morning made staying in his truck for the foreseeable future a viable third option.

He shouldn't have been there in the first place. He was supposed to go to his grandpa's home and finish packing up the old man's things. Half of his stuff was sitting in boxes while the other half was in its right place: the cutlery in a kitchen drawer, the wooden carvings on shelves, and the bed sheets still unmade from the last time his grandpa had slept there. Those would be the hardest to pack. Those might never leave the house. So there was still some packing to be done. Gideon thought of it all, perhaps as a distraction, to keep himself from going inside the hospital. There was still the cutlery and the carvings and the bed sheets, but there were other things, too, like the scribblers his grandpa had used to write on. And each box, once packed, had its own destination, instructions given explicitly to Gideon by his grandpa. The clothes, all of them, were to go to the Salvation Army in the city, the carvings distributed to whomever Gideon wished (and he could keep whichever ones he wanted), and the scribblers were to be thrown out. His grandpa hated them, and so did Gideon.

It was getting harder to remember his grandpa's voice, how confident it sounded when the old man imparted his wisdom, how comforting it was to Gideon, the low, melodic hum of it. It was only last fall when he'd gone out to his grandpa's house and found the old man panicking, unable to control his tongue, unable to swallow his breakfast without choking on each bite, unable to speak properly. "I thound ike a damn wee-thard," he'd struggled to say. And so the old man's voice, how it really was, was distorted by the memory of those first months, and how he struggled with the simplest words.

His grandpa's symptoms didn't get much worse in the early stages, when the sickness was still a mystery, and that was counted as a blessing. But, even still, there were changes. He lost a lot of weight because he couldn't eat any solid foods. Gideon had gone to Walmart and picked his grandpa up a bunch of Boost, pudding, and soup so that he'd get as much nutrients as he could, but it was impossible not to notice changes: how his clothes got baggier, and how his pot belly, which Gideon had used as a pillow when he was a kid, got smaller. And the old man talked less and less because he pronounced words like somebody was holding his tongue, and this embarrassed him. Gideon had made him laugh one day when he held his own tongue and said *apples* like his grandpa did. "Assholes, assholes, assholes," he kept saying until the old man cracked up. Those were rare moments of levity.

His grandpa was referred to an ENT at first, but the specialist wasn't able to figure out what was wrong, so he was referred again to a neurologist. After a series of tests, followed by days of anxiety for Gideon and his grandpa as they waited for the results, the news came, and the mystery was solved. The old man had ALS. Gideon didn't know what the hell that meant until the doctor told him it was more commonly known as Lou Gehrig's disease—everybody knew baseball facts around the rez. Once that news had been given, once they were told how hopeless the situation was, that there was no cure, it was as though the old man gave up, and the decline became rapid. He soon couldn't eat anything through his mouth, not even pudding or Boost, and he had to have his stomach hooked up to a machine that fed him what looked like baby food. His voice left entirely and he had to write in those damn scribblers. Gideon had got them for his grandpa. He'd gone to the school and they'd given him a bunch of them. They were all the colours of the rainbow.

It wasn't long before his grandpa had to be moved to the hospital, because doing things alone had become too difficult, and Gideon couldn't be there all the time. He'd be working the odd job, like helping to build the new arena, or, more recently, sandbagging, or he'd be over at Alice's place. He wasn't prepared to spend less time with the girls; they were as much his family as his grandpa was. And, besides, he wasn't trained to do the things that needed to be done to care properly for the old man. Rock bottom seemed to be redefined on a daily basis, but nothing could've been worse than the news he'd gotten this morning. The doctor had called to tell Gideon that his grandpa lost the use of his legs, just like that. Now the old man was in the hospital, unable to speak, eat, or walk. So Gideon stayed in his truck, his forehead pressed against the steering wheel, his thoughts leading him to any number of places, but no place he wanted to be. He wanted his grandpa back how he was, not like this. He already had images of his mother lying on her bed, looking like a sheet of skin placed over a sack of bones, so ravaged was she by the cancer and chemo. He didn't want the memories of his grandpa to be ruined as well.

You're selfish, though, god damn it, he thought to himself. What would his grandpa want? Would he want his grandson, the man he'd raised, sitting outside in his truck like a coward? What if it was Gideon in the room, alone, unable to speak, to walk, and scared? Gideon lifted his head, took a deep breath, and shut off the truck's engine. He thought of his grandpa's place, where there was a box full of photo albums. There were pictures of the old man in them. When the time came, he would look at them, he would memorize his grandpa's face how it used to look, he would stare at it until everything he'd come to know over the past several months was washed away. But what about the old man's voice? How would he remember that? Gideon shook his head. He'd never been one to videotape or record anything. His grandpa's voice would be lost. There was no way around it.

Gideon opened the door and stepped outside. He stood there for a moment, looking over the building, thinking how he never expected his grandpa to be there, never expected it to be a place he'd have to visit. The Elders' residence, sure. People got old. But he couldn't remember his grandpa ever being sick, and so the thought of him being in the hospital had never crossed his mind. He walked to the front entrance. Visitors were coming and going, people with sadness on their faces, their features loose and sunken, sadness in how they walked, their feet dragging across the gravel parking lot. He went inside.

Gideon walked past the reception desk and turned down the hallway to his grandpa's room. Innis General Hospital never felt much like a small-town hospital. In fact, he'd heard it was nicer than most of the hospitals in the city. It'd just been built in the past few years, and it was clean, bright, and comfortable. He was glad that his grandpa was there. As terrible as things had been, being where he was made things more manageable. And the staff, mostly people from the rez due to a nursing shortage, took good care of him. They'd even given him a room with a window—which, in there, was like getting the penthouse suite in a hotel—and seeing the sun was something the old man likely cherished.

Gideon saw Roxie, a short, stocky woman from the rez, leaving a room at the end of the hallway, probably his grandpa's. When he'd found out she was going to be his grandpa's primary caregiver, he didn't like the idea. He wanted the best for his grandpa, and all he knew about Roxie was that she was Gunner's "booty call" after late shifts at the Health Centre back home. Anybody who would go to bed with Gunner wasn't somebody Gideon wanted caring for his grandpa, even if he and Gunner had recently, more or less, patched things up. Patching things up with Gunner didn't mean he'd spend time with him, or that he thought much of people who did. But, after Gideon saw Roxie with his grandpa, how gentle and attentive she was (and gentle wasn't something he'd expected from somebody so husky looking), he gradually changed his mind. Now Gideon didn't want anybody but Roxie looking after his old man, and she could sleep with whomever she damn well pleased. He greeted her warmly as she passed.

"Hey, Roxie," he said.

"Hey, Gideon," she said.

"How's he doing?" he said.

She stopped walking, looked behind her, back to the room she'd just left, and kept her eyes there for a long while before turning back toward Gideon.

"He'll be happy you're here," she said.

Gideon thanked her, and she continued on her way. He walked to the end of the hallway and turned into his grandpa's room. The first thing he noticed was the white sheet, and how his grandpa's skin, once a strong, earthy brown, seemed to blend in with the bedding. For a moment he thought back to the shape of Grace underneath the white sheet in Alice's driveway, and then forced the image from his mind. When this was over, he never wanted to see another white sheet for the rest of his life. He used to have one over his futon back at his place, but after Grace died he threw it away, and since then he'd been sleeping in his clothes without anything covering him. His grandpa turned toward him and managed a weak smile, then turned back to face the window. The sun was in a perfect spot. The old man had put a dream catcher in front of the window the first night he stayed there. Its shadow now fell across his face, and it looked as though he was caught in a web. Gideon walked across the room and stood beside his grandpa's bed. He followed the old man's gaze out the window, where the sun hovered over the golf course.

Seeing the course reminded him of when he was a teenager and how he'd go down to Innis with his grandpa to golf. Gideon used to be a hot-tempered golfer. He'd broken more than one golf club in his day, and some of his clubs were probably still resting in the thick bush around the course. That all changed one day after Gideon had sent an approach shot about 50 yards right of the green following a perfect drive. He slammed his club into his golf bag so hard it broke his eight-iron. While he was stewing over his shot and his broken club, his grandpa calmly walked over to him. He looked into the bush, where, somewhere, Gideon's ball had landed.

"Now, lookit," he'd said. "There you are with a broken club, and you still have to find your ball wherever you hit it."

"So what?" Gideon said.

"So can you change the shot you just hit?"

"No," Gideon said.

"Okay then," the old man said. "Go find your ball and hit a good one. We can't change what's happened, we can only control what we do next."

Gideon waited a long time before his grandpa turned away from the window to his direction. When the old man did, Gideon smiled at him and tried his best not to look full of pity, but he failed. Truth was, there was plenty of it to go around. He felt bad for his grandpa; how, after all the years he'd been alive and how hard he'd worked, this was the hand he'd been dealt. It was plain shitty, and there was no other way to put it. But Gideon also felt bad for himself, and he wasn't sure if that was selfish or not, but it sure seemed that a lot of bad things had happened to him over the past year, and there weren't a lot of good things to balance things out. Grace had been killed, whoever ran her over had never been caught, and now his grandpa was dying. But he did feel bad for smiling like he did, because his grandpa didn't need that. Grandpa was the type of man to hate that kind of attention.

"How you doin'?" Gideon said.

His grandpa reached to the side of the bed and pulled out a yellow scribbler with a Bic pen stuck within the pages like a bookmark. He opened the scribbler, picked up the pen, and wrote down a few words. When he was finished, he passed the scribbler to Gideon and pointed at the words. Gideon was familiar with the routine. He'd been passed scribblers of all colours for a while now. He read the words.

"Pack any boxes this morn?" they spelled.

Gideon shook his head.

"I was kind of preoccupied," he said, and motioned to his grandpa's legs.

The old man grunted and grabbed the scribbler from Gideon. He aggressively wrote down more words then passed the scribbler back to his grandson.

"I want to know the work's done."

Gideon nodded.

"Okay, I'll do it," he said.

After the exchange, a silence fell between them, and, even after the time they'd spent together with the old man sick like he was, the quiet hadn't become less frustrating. Gideon had found ways to cope with it the best way he could; he would imagine things they might say to each other if they could talk like they used to. And so he imagined what his grandpa would say to him now.

"How's Alice doing?" he would ask.

"Oh, Alice, she's doing about as good as you could expect. You know, it's been about seven or eight months, but sometimes it feels like yesterday," Gideon would say.

"And the girls?" his grandpa would say.

"The girls, they're managing. Sometimes I think they go on like they always did, because kids are tough. But then, sometimes, you can tell how much they miss Grace," Gideon would say.

"You getting work?" his grandpa would ask.

He was always concerned that Gideon was working hard. He always expected people to work as hard as he'd worked all his life. How could they not? Working hard was all he knew.

"I've been sandbaggin', yeah," Gideon would say.

"That's good, Grandson, that's real good," his grandpa would say.

But his grandpa had not said anything, and the silence was still there, and it was torture. Gideon got a chair from the corner of the room and pulled it over to the side of the bed, and on its way it scraped against the floor, making the kind of nails-against-chalkboard sound that was typically unwanted but today welcomed. He wished the floor was longer and that the chair was louder. When he got to the side of his grandpa's bed, he sat down and leaned forward against it, resting his chin against his crossed arms, now at eye level with the old man. They shared a look, and perhaps it was just the moment, but for the first time Gideon saw sadness. With so much quiet between them for so long, Gideon had seen an array of emotions from his grandpa—frustration, anger, regret, even fear—but never sadness. And of all the emotions that had painted themselves against the old man's face, that was the most difficult to bear.

Gideon's body began to shake as he tried to hold back tears, but they wouldn't stay inside. He tried to hide them, even with his trembling body, as though his grandpa was blind, not speech-less. He buried his head into his arms and let the tears dampen his forearms and the damn white sheets on which they rested. Then he felt a cool, thin hand rest against his, and the touch was familiar. He remembered it from the first time there was silence. Gideon was 11, and had been living with his grandpa for about a year. A violent storm had come and left their house without power. For a long time, Gideon stayed in his bedroom, hidden deep under the covers, trying to escape from flashes of lightning, the cracks of thunder, the wind pushing up against his window, howling like an angry ghost. But he couldn't take it anymore. He got out of bed, crept across the house, went into his grandpa's room, and sat down on the floor beside the old man's bed. He pulled his legs into his chest, crossed his arms across his knees, and buried his head into his forearms. There was another flash of lighting and, instantly, a crack of thunder that sounded like it split the sky in two. The storm was right above them, bearing down on them. Gideon closed his eyes tighter, buried his face deeper, but his heart raced faster. Then he felt his grandpa's hand rest against his, and the storm seemed to subside, the lightning was not as bright, nor the thunder as loud, nor the wind as strong. He felt safe.

Gideon lifted his head to find his grandpa looking at him. He wiped the tears away and sat up straight.

"Thanks," he said.

His grandpa nodded.

"You know, I don't think I'll ever get used to this," he said.

The old man took his hand away. He opened the scribbler, picked up his pen, and started to write a message. Gideon watched the old man's face as he wrote. His eyes, thoughtful and intense, looked the same whether he was writing or speaking, and his brow was the slightest bit furrowed. Whenever the old man was think-ing, his brow would be furrowed. Gideon smiled. His grandpa had done so much thinking in his life that even when his brow was relaxed there was a deep line between his two eyebrows that never went away, and faint lines across his forehead like roads on a map. His grandpa stopped writing and pushed the scribbler across the bed. Gideon picked it up and read the words.

"You may not like it. I don't. But it is the way it is."

He closed the scribbler. Was it the words, or was it how he spoke them? Was it the voice? He couldn't help but think that, if his grandpa could talk, if he could hear the words, the old man would say something that would make everything okay. They would be like a cool, frail hand resting against his. Why couldn't they be spoken? God, please. Gideon looked over at the Bic pen and wanted to snap it in half. It wasn't the same and wouldn't ever be.

"Say something wise, Grandpa. Tell me something like you always did," he said, the tears coming again, and Gideon making no effort to stop them.

The old man opened his mouth, his eyes suddenly desperate, and let out an indecipherable grunt.

"Say something! Please!"

The old man tried again, but then shook his head and looked away, out the window. Gideon, tears soaking his cheeks, picked up the scribbler and threw it against the wall. The pages opened and it fluttered to the floor.

"Fuck you, then! Fuck you!" he screamed.

Roxie appeared instantly and stopped at the doorway to find Gideon staring at the scribbler on the ground near the foot of the bed and the old man staring at his grandson.

"Everything okay in here?" she said.

"Yeah," Gideon said without looking up.

His grandpa nodded.

"You sure?" she said.

Gideon looked over to her.

"Yeah, everything's fine. Sorry," he said.

Roxie took one last look, then left.

Gideon walked over and picked up the scribbler, then returned to his chair and sat down, placing the scribbler flat against the bed in front of him. He began to straighten it out as though it was a wrinkled shirt and continued the motion as he said, "I'm sorry, Grandpa, I'm just mad, y'know? It's not fair. It's just not fair."

The old man sighed, and then, almost against his will, reached over and took the scribbler. He picked up the pen and wrote, his eyes deep and intense, his brow scrunched together in thought. It took him a long time. Even in the short time Gideon had been there, the act of writing seemed more difficult by the moment. This was how the disease worked; his grandpa got tired faster, and more easily. The old man passed the scribbler to Gideon.

"Life's not fair or unfair, son. Life is life, and that's all we get," his grandpa had written.

The words were getting harder to make out, as though written by a child. Gideon thought about Jayne's writing as he looked at his grandpa's. There wasn't much difference. He read the words over and over again, and then tried to imagine the old man saying them. They were there, like a whisper, but there. But would they always be?

"I'm going to forget your voice. I want to remember your voice," he said.

For the last time, his grandpa reached over and took the scribbler. He wrote as slowly and as carefully as he could, fighting through the exhaustion he must have been feeling, the shaking hands and heavy arms. He needed rest. Gideon took the scribbler from his grandpa when he was finished.

"The words are my voice. The words are what matter."

The passage was read once, and then the scribbler was shut. Gideon looked the thing over, the piss-yellow colouring, the cheap, already frayed edges of paper, and the black, fancy letters that spelled Hilroy. Then he rolled it up and stuffed it into his back pocket. By this time the sun had moved from its place outside the window, and the dream catcher's shadow now spilled out across his grandpa's body, the webbed black lines making the white bedding look like a sheet of broken glass. The old man lifted his arm, straightened his hand, and reached out to his grandson. Gideon took his grandpa's hand and shook it, and, as he did, he remembered something the old man had said. He remembered it clear and crisp, as though his grandpa had spoken the words right then.

"You always shake hands, Grandson. It's what gentlemen do. You shake hands to thank somebody, to agree with somebody, to say you're sorry, to say hello, and, most of all, always, to say goodbye."

Gideon didn't get over to see his grandpa the next day, and couldn't be blamed for it. His day was busy. He'd spent it over at Alice's place, playing with the girls for the better part of the morning, and then, later, sandbagging homes, because the water kept rising and rising. But the truth was, he didn't feel like he could, even though, as hard as it was, he wanted to. It had taken him the entire evening to steady himself after he'd left the hospital, and he hadn't even felt right the next morning. He'd decided that he needed a break. Just for one day. So, he played with the girls as best he could, and sandbagged as hard as he could, even though, during both activities, his mind was elsewhere, either picturing his grandpa's face or trying to hear his voice speaking to him, saying the words that were written in the scribbler Gideon had taken with him. Some kind of break, he thought as he arrived home that evening. He fell asleep on his futon watching television with plans to visit the old man in the morning.

He woke up to the sound of his cell phone ringing, which he answered with his eyes still closed.

"Hello?" he said.

"Gideon?" Roxie said.

Gideon's eyes darted open.

"What is it?" he said.

"It's your grandpa," she said. "He..."

"Did he lose something else? Can he not move his arms or something?" he said.

"Gideon, he died this morning," she said.

Gideon sat up and ran his free hand through his hair. He pictured his grandpa's face, sunken, thin, tired. Would that now be the picture he had of the old man? He tried desperately to picture his grandpa before the illness but failed. He stood up and began to pace back and forth. Roxie didn't say anything for a little while, perhaps giving him time to process the news. Quiet was familiar. He'd learned to deal with it. In his mind, as he paced back and forth, lost in a world without his grandpa, the man who raised him, he flipped through the old man's scribbler and recited the words within it. But there weren't enough.

"You should come here. You should come to see him," Roxie said.

Gideon stopped pacing.

"Yeah, okay," he said. "I'll come by."

Gideon got dressed and left his house with his grandpa's scribbler carefully rolled up and placed in his back pocket. He got into his truck, turned on the engine, reversed out of the driveway, and started his way down the highway. Nothing seemed real. The houses at the side of the highway, the discarded items in the ditch, the waking sun, the rising waters, all felt distant and cloudy. He followed the highway's yellow dotted line, trusted it to guide him, because he didn't think he could get there on his own. If the old man were there with him, he would tell Gideon something wise, words that only he could say, and things would be clear, and he would know the way. But his grandpa wouldn't be there, not ever again. He was gone, and with him, his voice, that soothing baritone. But what about the words? What had he written?

Gideon stopped his truck suddenly, pulled a U-turn in the middle of the highway, and headed in the opposite direction. He ended up at his grandpa's place, where there were all the boxes waiting to be moved, and all the things that had yet to be boxed. He would pack them later, just as he had promised. The old man had wanted to know it was done, and it would be. The cutlery, the wood carvings, the bed sheets. But not the scribblers, piled up on the floor in the corner of the room. Gideon gathered them up and placed them on the coffee table in a neat stack, along with the one that had been in his back pocket. He didn't get over to see his grandpa that day. Instead, he spent his time opening scribbler after scribbler and reading what the old man had written.

"No, I don't wish I was younger. If I changed what I'd done, then I wouldn't have learned what I did."

"You want to see if I can't get two damn buckets of water?"

"I don't think heaven's a bunch of white clouds and string music. I think heaven's a trapline. It's green and brown and clear and simple."

"If you come late why do you think you can leave early? Get an alarm clock and leave at the same damn time."

And the words were all that mattered. The words were enough.

TEN

Later that morning, still hiding in their secret place, the old man and the boy sat down together on a large rock and looked out over the calm waters, across the sky's reflection, all the way to a small island cozied up against the horizon.

"Of course, Grandson, your daddy died well before your mom, and even before you were born. You know that. And you know, too, all the things I've told you about him over the years. When he was your age, he looked exactly like you. Talked like you, too. Anyway, I think you're old enough to know an important story about your daddy. You see, that island out there, it wasn't always called Widow's Island. It used to be called Bald Head, on account of how the trees only grow by the shoreline, never on the hill in the middle of the land. People and things get named for a reason. Widow's Island, it has a reason for its name too. Years ago, your mom and dad were out in the middle of the lake on their canoe— they always went canoeing around the area, and oftentimes all the way out to the island—when a storm came. It was a bad one, too. The rain was coming down real hard. Well, they were just about as far out as they were in, so they decided to keep on going to Bald Head because the trees out there, they're enormous, and they figured they could find some shelter.

"They got there without much trouble, even though the wind was kicking up something fierce. They were experienced on the water. So, they went and found shelter under the biggest tree they could find. Under that tree, they could hardly feel the storm at all. And you know what they did? They went and fell asleep. I'm not

kidding, Grandson. They were out there in the storm, under that tree, sleeping like babies. But all around them the storm got worse, and pretty soon there was thunder and lightning, and one of those bolts of lightning hit the tree they were sleeping under. Your mom, she got thrown almost to the water, like the island was spitting her out. Your dad, well, he took the brunt of that lightning strike.

"You know how I always told you that your dad died in an accident? Well, that right there was the accident. People've died worse, Grandson, but they've died better, too, and I know it's hard to hear. I guess if there was anything good about it, it was that your daddy died instantly. Didn't suffer, not even for a second. Your mom stayed with him. Said she lay down right beside him so they were face to face, and talked to him all through the night like he was still with her, like he was just sleeping. You know how we go to visit your daddy every now and then, and you sit there and tell him all about what you've been up to and how much you miss him? Well, he can hear you, Grandson. I'll tell you that much. Don't ever think he can't. And your daddy heard everything your mom told him that night, too.

"Well, that's how Bald Head got renamed Widow's Island. But you know what? That's not the end of the story. Pretty soon after that, after your mom was rescued and brought back to the mainland, she found out she was pregnant, and that was a miracle. She and your daddy had been trying to have a baby for years but they were never able to conceive one. Nine months later, out you popped. And Grandson, I know you might be wondering why I'm telling you this, today of all days. I guess I just want you to know that, sometimes, good things come from bad things."

RUNNING ON FENCES

HENRY STUMBLED DOWN THE STAIRS to the first floor, trying to rush but encumbered by a straight leg that made him feel like a pirate. The reason Henry had a straight leg was due to the stolen change in his pocket, otherwise known as his booty. You see, his wife had lowered an embargo on frivolous expenditures, and, unfortunately, Henry's craving for a grande double chocolate-chip frappuccino fell under the category of frivolity. For him, this simply wouldn't do, and since he was forbidden to spend his own money on frappuccinos he'd resorted to thieving from his son's piggybank. He figured he could sneak out of the house without getting caught by his wife (who had superhuman senses) by preventing the change in his pocket from rattling. And he would've made it without seeing his wife at all, if not for the mirror by the front door. He stopped there after retrieving his coat and made the mistake of gazing at himself, admiring the hold of the new pomade he'd bought. He was pleased with the results, delighted to find that, even though he'd put the stuff in his hair hours ago, it didn't need fixing.

"Henry."

"Shit," he whispered under his breath as Bev appeared from the kitchen.

"What did you say?" she said.

"Nothing. What's up?" he said.

"What are you getting at the store again?" she said.

She wasn't asking him because she'd forgotten, but rather testing him to ensure he'd remembered. If he failed to remember one item on the mental grocery list, he would get a handwritten grocery list. And, if Bev wrote out a list, there would inevitably be 10 to 15 more items on it, and that simply would not do. He'd have to spend more time at the grocery store and wait longer to get his drink.

"A loaf of bread, milk, and a fruit tray," he said confidently.

Bev stood there with her head tilted to one side, one eyebrow slightly raised, her arms crossed in front of her chest. For a moment, Henry became distracted. Her arms were too close to her breasts, perky and supple behind her delicately patterned floral apron. He looked her up and down after that, from her loose ponytail, where a few strands of hair had escaped and seductively fallen over the right side of her face, to her bare feet, which always drove him crazy. He'd had a thing for feet since the fourth grade, when he'd seen Stacey Snowden trace her naked foot with a red crayon. He saw Bev's foot tapping. She was waiting. He snapped out of it. What had he forgotten? Ah yes, clarification.

"A nice loaf of bread and homo milk," he said, which made him laugh. The word *homo* always made him laugh regardless of context.

"Okay," she said, suitably impressed, "but don't get the bread that you get, the sourdough kind. Nobody likes it but you. Get something delicious, but nothing with cheese in it, and no sourdough."

He nodded, leaned forward, and gave her a kiss.

"And please be on time. I need to start supper by…"

"Five, I know, hon," he said.

He turned away, all the while wondering how a loaf of bread that wasn't sourdough and didn't have cheese in it could be delicious at all. By then, he'd stopped worrying about the forbidden change. It was behaving in his pocket and he was sure Bev didn't suspect anything. And, at that point, if she did hear anything that might arouse suspicion, he would simply to tell her that she'd heard his car keys. He opened the front door and walked outside, feeling devious, brilliant, and happy to be met with a rush of crisp air. Travelling along the breeze, Henry swore he could smell a faint hint of double chocolate chip.

He made his way up the front walk toward his car. As he opened the gate, he noticed that the boy across the street—Juniper or Journey or some other kind of hippy name—was in the midst of doing what he always did: running along the top of his rickety fence, the top boards perilously shifting from one side to the other, the width of which couldn't have been more than that of a gymnastics beam. Juniper (or whatever) was as lithe as a gymnast, too. He ran from one end of the fence to the other, hopping over the gate in the middle of his little course without breaking stride. Henry stood there for a moment watching the boy and, like always, did so with a mix of awe and bewilderment. The boy was good, there was no question, but why the hell would he do such a thing, and how could he be so pleased doing it?

Henry didn't dwell on it long. After all, there were more important things on his mind. He walked across the boulevard, around the hood of his car, and into the driver's seat. He drove away from his house untroubled and determined to enjoy the drive just as much as he would his drink, even though the scenery wasn't all that pretty. It was, after all, spring, and that meant the snow had melted away and all the garbage it hid—the cigarette butts, the Slurpee cups, the beer cans, the dog shit, the McDonald's wrappers, and so on—was uncovered. Winter hid the secrets of the city. Spring was confession time.

He hadn't gone far when the phone rang. Before looking at the call display, he knew it was Bev. She'd forgotten something. The benefit of her remembering now as opposed to before he left, however, was that she couldn't write down a list for him. So, he answered the phone happily.

"Hey there," he said as he looked into the rear-view mirror to check his hair, which in itself was a useless exercise, done more by rote than by necessity; the current length of his hair coupled with the super-powered pomade he'd used made any follicle of hair moving even a fraction an impossibility.

"I have something to add," she said. "Are you going to remember?"

"I can remember five things, yes," he said.

"Can you get some pineapple, please?" she said.

"Aren't I already getting a fruit tray?" he said.

"I like to have my own pineapple," she said.

"Yeah, but the fruit tray comes with a compartment for pineapple, and me and the boy won't eat it. You can have it."

"Would you mind? Call it a quirk, but it's like you and your frappuccino drinks, only my quirk doesn't cost five dollars."

"Actually, they pretty much do cost five dollars," he said.

Henry could almost hear Bev roll her eyes.

"Pretty please?" she said.

"Fine. Okay," he said.

He wanted to ask why he couldn't get a frappuccino if she was getting pineapple but decided against it. He never really won an argument, and he was getting a drink anyway, albeit through underhanded means.

"So," she said, "what are you getting?"

"What I said before plus pineapple," he said.

"I'll text you a list," she said and hung up.

It wasn't until just before he reached the Salter Bridge that he received a text notification but decided to ignore it until he arrived at the grocery store at the very earliest, and possibly even later than that, if at all.

Traffic was slow; it took an eternity to get to the bridge's apex, and it was there, as he looked this way and that out of sheer boredom, that he noticed an Aboriginal woman standing on the walkway. He thought she was Aboriginal anyway, judging by her black hair, brown skin, and the distinctive features that were familiar to him from the news. He chuckled at the description he would have given of her if he were a reporter: Aboriginal in appearance. Those were common words to hear. She was of medium height, with blue jeans, Converse sneakers, and a hooded sweatshirt. He noticed these things only because, for one reason or another, the slow traffic had now stopped entirely. What caught his attention most was the young woman's eyes: big and brown, almost cartoonish, but striking all the same, and sad, most of all. It seemed that wherever she looked she was searching for something that was far out of reach. And, when she looked over at him and their eyes met, it was as though he had caught the sadness, as people catch each other's yawns, because he instantly felt a slight ache in his heart.

His windows were rolled down slightly, not because it was a particularly beautiful day out, but rather because he liked that others could hear the music he was playing. It made him feel relevant (he was listening to a hip, alt-rock band called The National). But the fact that his windows were rolled down gave him a passing thought that he should say something to the woman, and his lips even moved, but there wasn't anything he could think of saying. He was never good with strangers. His inability to say anything to the woman only solidified his feelings in that regard. Still, the sadness in her eyes was hard to ignore, and it was hard to look away from him. It was strange, too, that she was just standing there, as though caught in her own little traffic jam. He thought of Jasper (or whatever) on his fence, never ceasing to move, and compared that to the woman, who was stationary, and Henry could understand neither of them. What could she be doing? When the car in front began to inch forward, and Henry did in turn, he felt an impulse to ask her just that before it was too late. And why *was* she looking at him, out of everybody else? But he asked no such thing, and, as he gathered momentum, images of his grande double chocolate-chip frappuccino supplanted thoughts of the woman standing sadly at the side of the road.

Not that he had to, because there were only a handful of things in his basket and he was sure he'd got everything he was required to buy, but for his sanity's sake—because when he failed to do something just as Bev asked, there were subtle repercussions—he proudly looked over the groceries he had been sent for and was certain he'd not missed one thing. He made his way to the self-checkout aisle and fumbled to get the bar codes scanned. The fumbling was due to the proximity of the Starbucks and the rush to get there, but also the fruit tray, which was the most awkward thing to scan. He eventually paid for the groceries and excitedly walked up to the Starbucks counter with an abnormally large smile. The cashier, a pretty little thing with light-brown hair tied back into a loose ponytail, crystal-blue eyes, and a noticeable bounce in her step, as if to illustrate just how much she loved her job, greeted him at the counter.

"Hey there, what can I get for you?" she said.

It took a sizable amount of restraint not to make a flirtatious comment about what he really wanted. He was very much relieved that he'd spent so much time ensuring his hair was perfect, and was certain, as she smiled at him, that she thought he was as cute as he thought she was. He imagined for a moment that she had said to herself (in a kind of *of-all-the-Starbucks-in-the-city,-you-walked-into-mine* moment), "What a handsome man, his jet-black hair coiffed just so, his blue eyes like a reflection of the clearest sky."

"I'll have a grande double chocolate-chip frappuccino, skinny, no drizzle," he said about as smooth as a baby's skin, adding in the "skinny" and "drizzle" parts only because he thought it sounded refined, and he was out to impress her.

"Sure thing," she said, then turned away and began expertly constructing his drink.

He watched as she tapped her feet to some imaginary music while she blended the ingredients together. She was unfettered by the weight of life, young and carefree, and her body told this tale; her tight black pants accentuated slight but playful curves, and just visible above the collar of her shirt was a Dumbo tattoo—original and cute. He'd always hated oglers, yet there he was, subtly scanning her over from top to bottom. When his drink was ready, he sighed in disappointment. Getting the frappuccino should have been a triumphant moment; it should have gleamed in the grocery store lighting. But to Henry it paled in comparison to the girl—whom he knew now as Alexis based on her nametag—and he was upset that the experience was nearly over. She reached forward and handed him his cup.

"Grande double chocolate-chip, skinny, no drizzle," she said, and he noticed that each time she pronounced a word with the letter *l* in it a shiver rushed through his body.

When he accepted the drink from her he made sure to brush his fingers against hers, and even allowed this contact to linger a moment as he thanked her altogether too profusely. He left with every intention to return as soon as possible, and not so much for the drink. He would even be willing to "borrow" more money from his son to do so.

Henry barely noticed the road as he made his way back home, daydreaming as he was of other things. However, as distracted as he was on his drive, and it would have been safer if he had been texting in all honesty, it was impossible not to notice flashing lights from two police cars parked sideways to block off the bridge. Henry checked the clock and did a quick calculation of how much later he would be if he took another route. He knew Bev wanted to get started on supper by five—she always did—and if, for whatever reason, she couldn't, she got grumpy. He wanted no part of that. He drove up to the makeshift blockade, following cars ahead that angrily turned left or right to take their own detours, and on a whim he pulled over and got out of his car. He walked up to a police car and asked one of the officers what was happening.

"There's a jumper on the bridge," the police officer said.

"A jumper? Somebody wants to jump off the bridge?"

"Yeah, a jumper, like I said."

"Think you'll be letting cars get up there soon?"

In the next five minutes, Henry thought.

"Doubt it. She's just standing at the edge there, ready to go," he said.

"Who is it?"

"Just some Indian woman. They do it all the time, you know. Indians, not women."

Henry's mind flashed to the girl he had locked eyes with on top of the bridge, and he knew it was her. She'd looked so sad. Everything made sense.

"God," he said, "I saw that woman up there not more than 20 minutes ago, you know?"

"No shit," the officer said. "You know her?"

What if he did? He'd seen it in her eyes. She'd wanted to talk to him. Maybe he could talk to her now, talk her down, save her.

"Could I go up and see her?" he said.

The officer looked up at the bridge, then back at Henry.

"You really know her?" the officer said.

What would he say to her, though? What if he said something wrong and she jumped anyway? What if he got up there and didn't say anything at all? He could picture it now. He'd just stand there and watch her, just like he watched Journey (or whatever) up there on his fence doing whatever the hell he was doing. Henry would stand there, dumbfounded, and then she'd jump and that would be that and he'd feel guilty, even though she probably would've done it anyway.

"Sir?" the officer said.

He heard the officer say it himself. That's what Indians did. They jumped. What difference could he make? Even if he said something right, something perfect, she might jump anyway. Then where would he be, and for what? Henry shook his head. It was a no-win situation going up there.

"No, I don't know her. Just somebody I saw," he said.

Henry turned around and walked away. He checked the time: 4:56 PM. It was late anyway. It was far too late to do something. Somebody else would talk to her. The police had people for that, and they could talk to strangers without any trouble.

By the time he pulled up out front of his house, Henry had mostly forgotten about Alexis the Starbucks barista. Even the frappuccino, as delicious as it was, had tasted much better in theory than it did in practice. Imagination worked that way, though. He looked, with great concern, at the clock, which told him he was now 20 minutes late. There wasn't even time to sneak to the side of the house and throw the frappuccino cup into the trash. Instead, he shoved it underneath the driver seat. The next time he drove somewhere he would throw it into a trash can somewhere else in the city, as though disposing of a dead body. A perfect crime. Bev didn't do much driving anyway, and her finding it under the seat wasn't likely. He turned off the ignition and reached over to gather the groceries. He remembered then that he hadn't checked his phone for Bev's text, but it was too late, and doing so would simply be a small admission that he really had needed the list. He stepped outside.

The first thing he noticed was that boy, J … whatever, running along the top of the fence, his dirty, splintered feet pigheadedly finding balance with each step, his matted blonde locks joyously whipping back and forth. Henry shook his head as he walked around the front of his car. The kid didn't get anything out of running on fences, except perhaps bumps and bruises that came from the odd fall. Henry felt bad for the boy—that was that. He'd probably end up running on that fence until he was an adult, always looking for a purpose and never finding it. He would probably end up like the Aboriginal woman he'd seen today, his naked toes dangling over the ledge, and the regrets of a misspent youth pushing him forward to a welcomed end. Maybe one day Henry would talk to the boy as he should have talked to the girl.

For the time being, however, Henry turned away, toward his house, where he saw Bev waiting at the front door, tapping her foot impatiently, her head tilted curiously, her arms crossed. He was already planning out what he would say. What could he have done to help it? He didn't intentionally come home 20 minutes late. He walked up to his wife and, before she could say anything, said, "There was a girl, an Indian girl, on the bridge trying to jump."

"*Aboriginal* girl," she said. "*Indian* is so offensive."

"But they call themselves that," he said.

"That doesn't matter, Henry. You can't call them that. They hate it when people call them that," she said.

"Anyway, that's why I was late," he said.

"Couldn't you just have gone another way?" she said.

"I did go another way," he said, "but before that, I don't know, I thought I could help her. I was sure I could help her."

"Help her? How?" she said.

"I'd seen her on the way to the grocery store. She wasn't about to jump then, mind you, but she looked upset about something. We met eyes and there was this weird connection, you know? Anyway, then, on the way back, I found out that the same girl was trying to jump and I thought I could maybe talk her down. So, I got out of my car and tried to get up there but the police wouldn't let me."

Bev gasped. "Oh my god, Henry, I hope she didn't jump. I hope to god she didn't jump when you could've saved the poor thing!"

"I know," he said and shook his head. "Let's watch the news after supper and we'll see if we don't hear something about it."

"Okay," she said.

Henry began to walk past Bev when she stopped him and gave him a hug. Deep in her embrace, he said, "I'm sorry I'm late. I know you wanted me home earlier."

"It's okay, hon. I mean, look what you had to go through," she said.

She squeezed him harder, and he turned his head to the side and kissed her on the neck.

"You know what I'm going to do?" she said. "I'm going to get you one of those drinks you like after supper."

When Bev eventually let him go, Henry walked inside the house, kicked off his shoes, and made his way into the kitchen. Then, one by one, he placed the groceries onto the kitchen counter: a fruit tray, a carton of milk, and a loaf of sourdough bread.

ELEVEN

When Matthew was in grade nine, he found an old dusty box in the basement storage room while he was looking for his collection of Spider-Man comic books, which his mom had hidden for no good reason. When he opened the box, he found that it was his old Culture In a Box project he'd done in elementary school. He'd forgotten all about it. He opened it and sifted through all the Scottish items: the family crest his father had printed from Google Images, a family tartan also printed out from Google that reminded Matthew of toffee and made him want some, and a tam o'shanter. He eventually found the Indian stuff. He took out a pair of moccasins and marvelled at the delicate beadwork, how it so perfectly illustrated howling wolves; a braid of grass that smelled wonderful, earthy and sweet; a small ceramic bowl and a bundle of sage attached to it with an elastic; and a small red box in the shape of an octagon that read Mother Earth Tobacco. He couldn't remember the significance of everything, but he inspected each one of them thoroughly. He felt so Indian all of a sudden, and proud of it, too. The only other time he had felt Indian was back in December. Tara, a girl he liked, had come up to him at school while he was placing books into his locker.

"Matthew, are you an Indian, or do you just have a tan?" Tara said.

Matthew shut his locker and leaned against it. He thought about what to say long enough to appear as nervous as he felt, then said, "I'm not an Indian."

"Oh, cool," she said. "So where do you go?"

"For what?" he said.

"For your tan," she said. "My mom takes me to this place that turns my skin orange every time."

Matthew responded with the only tanning place he could think of. He'd heard commercials while listening to Jets games. "Fabutan," he said.

"Really? Hmph. I never go to cheap places, and look at your skin. Just look at it. It's fucking perfect."

At the time, he'd left Tara feeling good. And while her skin turned more and more orange in the weeks following, she'd remained enamoured with his perfect little "tan," and he liked the attention. He felt differently about it now, though. He looked the items over, one by one, as he placed them back with his Culture In a Box project, saving the moccasins for last. He turned them around in his hands, thinking about how comfortable they must have been and wishing he could wear them, but they were altogether too small. Before putting them away, he placed one moccasin beside his forearm. He looked back and forth between his skin and the leather, comparing colours.

FUTURE DAYS

GIDEON WAS SITTING IN THE LOBBY of his therapist's office wondering why he'd moved to the city in the first place. When he'd made the decision, it seemed like the right one, maybe the only one. Bad things had kept piling up for him just as the waters around the rez continued to rise. There'd been Grace's death, of course, and the fact that whoever ran her over still hadn't been found. And then, after Grace, his grandpa got sick and had just recently passed away. But it felt like it'd all come to a head when Alice and the girls disappeared, and right after his grandpa's death. He still remembered when he'd gone to Alice's place to see her and the girls after they hadn't shown up at his grandpa's wake. It was like somebody had just swooped them up and taken them right in the middle of breakfast.

When he'd seen the unoccupied kitchen table, and the cold bacon and eggs on all the plates, his body got all numb and tingly. Later, he'd describe the sensation as being "kinda like the feeling coming back to your arm after you slept on it." Despite that unpleasantness, he rushed through the house and checked in every room to make sure they weren't holed up somewhere else, but every room was empty. As he was walking down the hallway back to the kitchen, his heart started to pound out of his chest, like he'd just run a few miles. Then, when he got to the kitchen, he found it tough to breathe, like a big fat person was sitting on his chest. He ran out onto the driveway and collapsed. Black spots came across his vision like rain and then everything shut off. Before he lost consciousness, he thought that was it for him, that he was having a heart attack.

Turned out, it was his brain giving out on him. That's how he understood it anyway. When it kept happening, and in the oddest places, too, like when he was sitting around his living room watching television, the doctor at the health centre figured Gideon needed therapy. The only thing was that the kind of therapy he needed wasn't available in the rez—he needed to go to the city for it. Now, he'd never cared very much for the city, but moving there was more appealing than staying around all the bad things. Of course, he knew Alice was living there. She'd been thinking about moving to the city ever since Grace died. But he told himself that wasn't why.

He had managed to find his way to the office, but only after getting lost and asking for directions at a coffee shop. He'd never really been anywhere in the city except for the Walmart right near the perimeter. He could navigate his way there, no problem. But walking around downtown was like trying to complete one of the mazes Jayne liked to do in her activity books. When he took wrong turns he found dead ends and had to back up and try a different way. It was loud, too. There was an incessant noise, a collision of car horns, rumbling engines, screeching tires, and shouting. It made the lobby seem more appealing than it might normally have been. It was simple and stress-free. There was a leather chair he was sitting in, some kind of exotic plant, an elegant side table, a magazine rack stocked with *Sports Illustrated, Time,* and *Maclean's,* and a calming selection of Baroque music playing. There was nowhere to get lost.

After a short while, the classical music was interrupted by the sound of footsteps approaching. Gideon turned to see a native man emerge from the hallway. He was clean-cut, dressed in a sky-blue dress shirt and pleated black pants with fancy black sneakers, comfortable but stylish, and had long hair tied into a perfect braid. He met Gideon with an outstretched hand and a smile.

"Gideon?" the man said as he shook Gideon's hand.

"Yeah, that's me," Gideon said. "How're you doing?"

"I'm great, never been better," the man said.

He followed the man out of the lobby and down a warmly lit hallway that was decorated with oil paintings of red flowers and orange fish.

"So, I'm glad you got here on time. Must've been a pretty long drive," the man said as they walked.

"Oh, I came out yesterday. Gonna live out here for a bit," Gideon said.

"Oh?" the man said. "Why's that?"

"Just needed a change, I guess," Gideon said.

"That's fantastic," said the man. "How are you finding your stay so far?"

They stopped at a door. The man opened it, and Gideon walked inside with him.

"Not sure yet," Gideon said. "The city wasn't this big, lookin' at it from the perimeter. It kinda makes me feel small, you know."

"You'll get used to it," the man said. "You'll grow."

They sat down across from each other, a coffee table between them. Gideon surveyed the office. There was a tiny potted plant on a bookshelf behind the man—a bonsai tree, Gideon thought. Beside the plant, there was a smattering of neatly placed book—titles like *Mindfulness and Acceptance, Book of Anxiety, Things Might Go Terribly, Horribly Wrong, I'm Okay You're Okay,* and EMDR. There was also a small throw rug with a soaring eagle stitched into it, a desk with nothing on it except a pen holder, and a portable air purifier.

"Well, let's get to it," the man said. "My name is Don, by the way."

Don opened a folder. He read through a few notes scrawled onto a leaf of yellow paper, said hmm a few times, and closed the folder again. He placed the folder on the coffee table. Gideon watched the folder as he would a television set, wondering what was written down on the yellow paper, what things it said about him.

"Gideon," Don said.

Gideon looked up. He already liked Don. There was something comforting about him. When he had been referred to see a therapist he was hesitant. He equated therapy with craziness, figured most people did. But Don made him feel a bit more at ease about the whole thing.

"The paper talks about what happened to you, but I'd rather hear it from you," Don said.

"What does it say happened to me?" Gideon said.

"That you had a panic attack," Don said.

"Yeah, I heard them call it that, too," Gideon said. "That all that's in there?"

"I think you'll explain things much better than a piece of paper could," Don said. "Do you want to tell me about the day you had the panic attack?"

"I guess so," Gideon said. He paused for a moment. He wasn't used to opening up about much of anything. But, when he met eyes with Don, who sat patiently and calmly, he felt encouraged to speak. Yes, he sure did like Don. He would be easy to talk to. There were only two people who he ever felt he could talk to before meeting Don. But his grandpa had passed on, and since Grace's death Alice hadn't cared much to hear Gideon say anything. He told Don about what had happened the day he went to Alice's house during his grandpa's wake. He described the feeling in his chest, the heaviness, and the pounding heart. He described how his entire body felt like it was in chaos.

"You thought you were going to die," Don said.

"Yeah, like I was having a heart attack or something," Gideon said.

"That's normal for what you experienced," Don said.

"Yeah?" Gideon said.

"Oh, yes," Don said. "It's very common to fear death when you're having a panic attack. Especially if you haven't experienced one before."

For the rest of the session, Don continued to delve into Gideon's history, about his family, his grandfather's death, his relationship with Alice and her two girls, and Grace's death and how it seemed to change just about everything. Gideon answered each question dutifully. At the end of the session, Don walked Gideon to the front door, where beyond lay the enormity of the city, and the expanse made Gideon feel uneasy once more. He turned to Don with a bit of desperation.

"So," said Gideon, "you think you can cure me?"

"I think I can help," Don said as he gave Gideon a warm pat on the shoulder, "there are things we can do."

"Like what kind of things? You gonna shock me or something?"

"Oh, dear, no. Not at all," Don said. "Why don't you let me worry about all that for now. Come back in two days. In the meantime, if you feel an attack coming on, take some deep breaths, in through your nose, out through your mouth. Exhale longer than you inhale. That will help calm you."

Gideon nodded, and with one of those deep breaths, as though he was about to jump into the deep end of a pool, he walked outside.

Walking home from his appointment, Gideon took a wrong turn and ended up finding refuge in a department store. The sense of relief didn't last long. The store was like a microcosm of the city, the twists and turns, the size of it, the noise. He wandered around the first floor for a long while and passed by the same section a few times. One of those sections was the perfume area. The smell made him want to vomit. He would have given anything, at that point, to be in Alice's trailer, sitting beside her, breathing in whiffs of her menthol cigarette smoke. Even that smell was much easier to take. Eventually he made his way up an escalator to the second floor. It was just as confusing there, but there were areas he was interested in—a sports section and a men's clothing section. He spent most of his time in the clothing section, daydreaming about the pants or shirts he would buy if he could afford it. It was hard to afford anything on $750 per month.

After the first few minutes in the menswear section, Gideon noticed a nice-looking woman going wherever he went. He began to glance at her as much as he glanced at the clothing. She had brown, shoulder-length hair, milky white skin, and was wearing a sleek black business suit. It was strange to see her there. Not that you never see a woman in a menswear section, because she certainly could have been looking at clothes for a father or a husband, but she didn't seem to be looking at clothing at all. Instead, she was looking at Gideon, glancing at him as much as he was glancing at her. When he stopped to look at a jacket that he particularly liked, a black leather jacket with a built-in hooded sweatshirt, she got even closer, and he could see a gold nametag that read Susan. She ended up standing in front of him, only the jacket between the two of them.

"Hey," Gideon said.

"Hi there," Susan said.

She didn't say anything immediately afterward, and it made Gideon feel a little uneasy. He tried to ignore her, to keep inspecting the jacket, but found it next to impossible. In an attempt to ease the awkwardness, he lifted the jacket up to show Susan and nodded at her with a smile.

"Nice jacket," he said.

She nodded, but without a smile.

"Sir, do you think that might be a bit out of your price range?" she said.

"Oh, I don't know," Gideon said. "I didn't even look at the price tag."

She took the jacket from him, which caught him a bit off guard. He watched as she placed the jacket back on the rack, then stood there silently, her hands crossed in front of her. He reached for the jacket again, but she stepped in his way.

"Can I look at it please?" Gideon said.

Susan shook her head.

"I think you should leave unless you plan on buying something," she said.

Gideon looked her over, from her shiny black shoes with the slightest hint of toe cleavage, her shiny white skin, her perfectly ironed pants and blazer, all the way to her smug smile, which was all the more pronounced by her bright pink lipstick. He wanted to say something, to defend himself, but the words wouldn't come. Then he felt his chest begin to get heavy, and he reached out and braced himself against a rack of windbreakers.

"Do I have to call security?" she said.

Gideon shook his head. He turned away and walked quickly toward the escalator. The farther he got away from Susan the better he began to feel, which was a good thing, too, because it took him just about forever to find his way out of the store and he didn't want to have a panic attack inside a building like that. When he got outside, he took two long breaths of air exactly as Don had instructed and managed to gather himself. There was a Tim Horton's across the street, and he could've really used a coffee, but he knew expenditures like that weren't the smartest thing. There wouldn't have been a point to buy something he could get back at his place anyway. He'd bought a package of cheap instant coffee from Walmart on his way into the city. No, if he was going to spend money on anything, he would've much rather gone back and bought that jacket just to show Susan a thing or two. But with the money it probably cost, he thought for sure he would end up living on the street. So there was no point doing that either. In fact, quite the opposite of showing her anything, he would've ended up right where she expected him to be already. He could picture her passing by him on the street and giving him the same smile she gave him inside the department store.

That night, an unexpected vibration from his cell phone interrupted Gideon's last bite of canned spaghetti. He hadn't received a text or phone call in quite some time because the only person who ever bothered to get a hold of him was Alice, and she'd vanished without so much as a goodbye. When he checked his phone, then, he was surprised to see a short text from Alice that read, "You wanna see me an grls?" After reading it, he snapped the phone shut, opened it, and shut it again. He thought, once more, about why he had moved to the city. Had it really been to get away from the bad things, or was it because he knew Alice was here? And if it was, why was his chest getting heavy, his heart starting to race? She'd just invited him over, for God's sake. Wasn't that what he wanted if he'd followed her here? He breathed in through his nose and out through his mouth. He did this five times until his body calmed.

He read the text over again as he chewed on his last bite of dinner. He chewed for much longer than he needed to, until the food felt more like tomato soup in his mouth than spaghetti. Where were they staying? Were they close? He read the text over as he rinsed out his dishes. Why would she leave without saying anything, and then ask to see him now? Did she think he was just here at her beck and call? He recited the text aloud as he stood on the balcony overlooking Central Park. He thought about the girls. They must've asked Alice about him. Their Uncle Gideon. He imagined the park was the field behind Alice's house, and he pictured Kathy and Jayne running through the long grass, their laughter replacing the angry downtown traffic. Why did she wait so long to text him? He walked back inside his apartment and plunked down on the futon. He opened his phone, began to write a text back, then closed the phone sharply. No, he couldn't see her or, as much as it pained him, the girls. Not now, not yet. He tossed his cell phone onto the floor and lay down and tried to go to sleep.

He was dreaming. He was out in the big field behind Alice's trailer. He was standing beside the tire swing and Alice was pumping her legs, swinging back and forth joyously and high. He could hear the girls laughing with staccato delight, their unabashed happiness carried to his ears through a gentle breeze. It was exactly the kind of moment that was too perfect to be real. As the warm breeze enveloped his body like another layer of clothing, he felt the dichotomy of a chill across his body. Against his will, he was pulled out of the dream and began to hazily open his eyes. He was stuck in the void between sleep and consciousness, not sure if he was in the midst of a dream or reintroducing himself to reality, when Gideon saw the figure of a woman standing in the middle of the room. She was facing him.

"Alice?"

He lifted his head up slowly, still transitioning into consciousness. When he did, the figure broke into a quick but graceful walk. She walked out of the room and toward the entryway. The woman's sudden movement jolted Gideon awake. He jumped off the futon and chased after her, but just as quickly as she was there, she was gone. He opened the door and ran out into the hallway. It was empty. He stood there for a moment, bathed in silence, hoping to see her, or, at the very least, hear a door shut, or the elevator ding. Nothing. He walked back into his apartment and checked the clock: 9:30 AM. His appointment with Don was in an hour, and there was just enough time to get there on foot. He grabbed his coat and walked out the door.

"What do you think is causing the panic attacks?" Don said.

"Alice," Gideon said. "You know, I'm not the smartest man you ever met, but I can connect the dots. I know my grandpa died and all, but I knew he'd go sometime. Alice, I didn't ever expect she'd be gone like that. It has to be her, somehow."

"What do you think it is about her?" Don said.

"I don't know," Gideon said. He paused for a moment, then added, "You know, she texted me last night."

"Really. Has she contacted you before? I mean, since she left like she did?" Don said.

"Nope, not a word," Gideon said.

"That's interesting," Don said.

Gideon thought it was funny Don said that. Before meeting Don he had a notion of what he thought a shrink would look like, would talk like, the things they would say. Don didn't really fit into any of that until just now. He'd always thought a shrink would say things like "that's interesting." Television was right sometimes.

"And did you text her back?"

"No," Gideon said. "I didn't want her to think I was gonna be there for her no matter what, you know? I'm not some house pet."

"But aren't you going to be there for her?" Don said.

Gideon shook his head, but thought the exact opposite. Of course, if she needed him, he'd be there for her. It didn't matter how mad he was at her. She was family.

"Here's what I want you to do," Don said. "Consider getting in touch with her. It might just help you start to get over this."

"Then I'll be cured?"

Don hesitated for a short while.

"A lot has happened to you, Gideon. You've let things build up, and your body is rebelling. It's trying to tell you that. What we're going to do is help you deal with things better. And, if we do that, yes, you might start to feel better."

That was enough for Gideon to consider texting Alice back, and it was all he needed to hear that day. Before the appointment, he had a mind to tell Don about the woman he'd seen in his apartment, but decided against it. For all he knew, it could've been somebody who'd broken into his apartment, and that was hardly a therapy thing. And, if it was something else, well, he didn't want Don to think he was nuts.

That night, Gideon had another dream. He was running down a driveway back at the rez. He could see a house at the end of the driveway, but no matter how far he ran he never got closer. There was a car outside the house. A sedan. The engine was on. He could see clouds of black smoke escape from the exhaust. He ran faster. Faster. The car peeled out of the driveway, kicking up dust in its wake. Gideon could see a figure sitting on the step behind the dust cloud. It was holding something. Faster. Faster. When the cloud settled, the house was closer. Gideon saw his grandpa, and sitting on his lap was Grace.

Gideon woke up with a start, gasping for breath. He wiped some sweat away from his brow and rolled over onto his side with the intention of getting up and heading to the bathroom to splash cold water on his face. That's when he saw the same woman from yesterday morning, lying in the middle of the floor. She had beautiful dark skin and ebony strands of hair. Her big, bold eyes were open and staring upward. He followed her gaze to the ceiling, on which there was nothing to see. He got up from the futon as quietly as he could. She didn't seem to notice him, kept staring at the ceiling. When he stepped forward, however, her eyes snapped away from the ceiling to look directly at him. It caught Gideon off guard. He stumbled back onto the futon. When he stood up, the woman was gone again. He ran to the entryway. The door was closed.

Without changing from the clothes he'd fallen asleep in, Gideon stormed down to the main office. The landlord greeted him with a middling little grin.

"Good morning," the man said. "How can I help you? Uhh, Gideon, right?"

"I think somebody has a key to my room," Gideon said.

The man looked at him curiously. He raised his eyebrows, and his entire head of hair moved unnaturally. Gideon had never seen a toupee before.

"There's only one key," the landlord said.

"What about whoever stayed in the room before me?" Gideon said.

"Oh," the landlord said. He looked as though he was going to say more, then stopped himself and said, quietly, "That's not possible."

Gideon stood there and tried to look as annoyed as he could. He wanted something more. He wanted anything.

"So you're sayin' you're not gonna do anything then?" he said.

"I'm saying there's nothing to do."

Gideon went for a long walk that afternoon. With each walk he'd become more familiar with the area. The city became less frightening to him. He found himself, for some reason, looking for Alice, scanning each passing stranger's face as though he might happen upon her. He knew he wouldn't see her, of course. He wasn't so naïve. Rather, the act of looking for her was more a distraction from the perplexity that was the woman in his apartment. He took in information as he scanned faces, glancing observations, and then casually let that information fall away: a man with a beige windbreaker carrying a yellow shopping bag and walking a dirty poodle—gone; a woman with inch-thick glasses, a tattered purple overcoat and a beret asking people for two dollars and crying horrendously, like a spoiled toddler, when coming up empty-handed—gone; a group of perfectly groomed men laughing perfectly groomed laughs walking out of an adult toy and clothing store—gone; a lanky olive-skinned thirty-something woman listening to an iPod walking onto Ellice Avenue without looking and almost getting hit by a Lincoln Navigator—gone; a woman pushing a baby grasping a bottle filled with cola in an umbrella stroller—gone. None of the faces, none of the people he saw, matched Alice's in the least. He decided he would text her later, invite her over anytime she could come. He spent the rest of his walk thinking of the best words to use.

When Gideon entered his apartment that evening, he instantly noticed the orange streetlight glow pushing in through the curtains on the sliding door that led out onto the balcony. It took him a moment to notice the cold because he'd just come in from outside. It took him a moment longer to notice the curtains gently flapping in the breeze. The sliding door was open. Gideon was sure when he'd left in the morning it was closed. He walked toward the curtains, which were dancing prettily, just like hair rhythmically whipping around in the wind. At one point, in the midst of a strong gust of wind, the curtains flew up toward the ceiling and revealed a clear view of the balcony. His heart stopped when he saw the silhouette of the woman standing there, facing away from him as though watching the activity in Central Park. The curtains fell back into place. Gideon rushed out onto the balcony, but the woman was gone. He spun around slowly, taking in every last inch of scenery, trying to catch a glimpse of her anywhere. It was no use.

"What do you want from me?" he said.

He turned toward Central Park and leaned over the railing. He looked out over the large field, which had an entirely different feel in the night than it did in the day, populated not by children and their toys but, instead, adults and their curiosities. The splash pad was littered with teenagers shouting boorishly, strung out across the metal jungle. He looked to either side of the park, where traffic still busily went on its way, oblivious to his troubles. He looked down to the sidewalk, where he saw only one person. A woman. Lonely. Sad. Her whole body was slumped over, and, to Gideon's surprise, she was looking right up at him. It wasn't the woman who kept showing up in his apartment. Even in the dark he could tell she had lighter skin, a thinner frame. His eyes lingered on her for a moment before she turned and walked away. Gideon went back inside, firmly shutting the sliding door. He made sure it was locked.

Before going to bed, he sent Alice a text that read "Come by any time you want," in part because Don had suggested that he do so, and he was determined to do whatever Don asked of him. But there was something else, too. Seeing the woman like he'd been seeing her made him feel like he was losing his mind. He needed somebody to talk to, and, as much as he trusted Don, somebody who wasn't there to analyze him, somebody who'd just listen. Alice never said anything much after Grace's death. She'd always just sat quietly and let Gideon talk. It didn't really matter if she was listening anyway. He could think she was and that would be fine. He waited up for a long time that night, hoping for his phone to buzz a text notification, but none came, nor did one come the next day. He wasn't upset about this. After all, he had not texted her back right away, and Gideon felt he deserved nothing better. He was disappointed, though. The girls certainly would've been a welcome distraction too. They always were. He would have been more than happy to play tea party with them, make paper airplanes, or even dress up like princesses.

After a silence that had stretched far too long, Don leaned back in his chair and sighed. He reached over and picked up a bottle of 7UP, untwisted the cap, filling the office with a refreshing fizz sound, and took a long sip. Once the pop bottle had been set down, Don placed a finger against his temple and smiled at Gideon.

"Okay," he said.

Gideon waited for Don to say something else, but no other words came.

"Okay, what?" Gideon said.

"What's on your mind?" Don said.

Gideon shook his head.

"You haven't said a word since you walked in, and honestly Gideon, you're here to talk," Don said.

"I don't have any words I want to say," Gideon said.

"Nothing? What about Alice? Did you send her a message back?" Don said.

"Yeah, but I don't have much to say about that," Gideon said. "She didn't text back anyway."

"How did that feel?" Don said.

"I didn't expect her to so it doesn't matter. That's not what I'm thinkin' about anyway," Gideon said.

Gideon looked down at the floor.

"You're gonna think I'm crazy," Gideon said. "You're only gonna think I'm crazy and stupid."

Don leaned forward.

"Believe it or not, despite my profession, I don't think anybody is crazy."

"Even still, I think I might be the first person you think is crazy," Gideon said.

"How about you tell me what's on your mind, and we'll go from there," Don said.

Gideon shifted uncomfortably in the comfortable love seat.

"I been seeing this woman in my apartment," Gideon said. "I mean, I been seeing her and I don't think she's really there."

"What makes you think she's not really there?" Don said.

"Because she's there and then she's not there," Gideon said.

"Let's start here: what does this woman do?" Don said as he thoughtfully sipped at his 7UP again.

"She's just kind of there, you know," Gideon said. "She's standing around, lyin' down on the floor, whatever. This morning I got out of the shower, and she was kind of just standing there like she was waitin' to hand me a goddamn towel or something."

"Have you tried to talk to her?" Don said.

"One time, but she doesn't say anything. Never says anything whether I'm talkin' to her or not."

"Could she live there? I mean, in the building?" Don said.

Gideon shifted his position again and the leather made a crunching sound. "I told you. She kind of just disappears. You know, into thin air."

"You mean, she is standing there and then, poof, she's gone?" Don said.

"No, she kind of just darts off and when I follow her she's gone," Gideon said.

"Well, could it be that she just, you know, leaves?" Don said.

Gideon thought about when he had seen her on the balcony. She disappeared there, too, and she sure as hell didn't jump, but maybe he'd imagined it. His head wasn't right after all. That's why he was seeing a shrink, wasn't it? Gideon shrugged.

"Lately I been kind of wanting to see her, too, you know," Gideon said. "At first I didn't wanna see her, and then I started to want to."

"Are you curious about her?" Don said.

"I guess," Gideon said. "Maybe."

"What happens before you see her? Does anything stand out?"

"No, not really. I seen her after a dream, after a walk, after a shower, whatever. She kinda just comes and goes as she pleases, you know," Gideon said.

Don looked Gideon over. If Gideon were to use Don's language he would say that Don looked as though he was processing.

"Would you call me if you see this woman again? I'll come over and we can talk about it. That might help us whittle things down a bit," Don said.

Gideon nodded. He patted his chest. There was a weight lifted. As they walked down the hallway, Gideon said to Don, "I guess the good thing is I haven't had any of them panic attacks."

"That is good, Gideon. That is very good."

Gideon walked home that day through the heart of the city, the alleys and avenues, the tributaries. Although he'd now negotiated his way throughout downtown's blood vessels on several occasions and felt relatively familiar with the area, he still felt alien to it, alone within it, and very small, like a solitary blood cell. And in that unfamiliarity he once more sought out a certain kind of comfort, a face that he would recognize. Only this time, unconsciously, it wasn't Alice's face he searched for, but rather the woman who visited him on occasion. He inspected each face that passed by. Some faces returned his curious stare with an awkward smile, others looked at him with a great deal of annoyance, others still with anger, but none of the faces matched the one he sought. It was when passing an old pub at the outskirts of the exchange district called the Yellow Dog Tavern that he saw somebody familiar, but not the woman in his apartment, and not Alice.

He stopped outside on the sidewalk just out of the woman's view. He looked her over carefully. Who was she? Perhaps one of the many faces he had passed during his walks through downtown. He went through them as best he could, one by one, but no faces matched. Another tenant? He'd seen a few faces here and there, although he didn't walk around the building too much. There was never a need to. The weight room had one broken treadmill, an elliptical machine the landlord was always on, his head glistening with sweat as he watched talk shows, opting not to wear his toupee while exercising, and a row of weights beside a rickety workout bench. The swimming pool had been closed down long before Gideon moved in. An old man in the elevator had told him it was because a young girl got her hair stuck in the drain a year previous and almost drowned. None of the tenants looked remotely like the woman in the Yellow Dog Tavern. Then it hit him. It was the woman he'd seen on the sidewalk staring up at his apartment.

Gideon walked inside the tavern as though drawn there. The woman was sitting by the window, facing outside, but didn't seem to be looking at anything in particular. She was alone, an empty chair beside her. Gideon walked up to the bar, ordered a diet drink, and made his way over to the woman. When he sat down beside her, she let out an annoyed sigh and took a quick sip of her beer. She didn't look over at him, kept looking outside. Gideon took a sip of his drink and faced the outside with her, but, instead of looking through the glass, he watched her reflection, which, in the gathering darkness, was clear. She had no makeup on. Her eyes were sunken, her hair hinted at prettiness but was tangled and worn, and the lines of her skin wrote the story of a difficult life. He took another sip of his drink. She twisted the beer glass around with her delicate fingers.

"What're you drinking there?" Gideon said.

She didn't answer, just took another sip of the anonymous ale.

"I don't drink, me," he said.

"Good for you," she said, and might as well have said those words to nobody. They were empty, just like her eyes.

"I seen you the other day, on the street outside my apartment building," he said.

She returned to her silence, pushed some hair behind her ear, shifted her body a bit farther away.

"You were lookin' up at me," he said.

"Where the hell was that?" she said.

Gideon said, "On Cumberland. That big ol' brick apartment block, you know. It's just down the street a ways from here."

They sat there in silence for a good while. She kept looking out the window, and he kept looking at her reflection. He expected her to get up and walk away.

"Oh," she said. "Well I wasn't looking at you."

She took a long drink, then placed the glass back. She ran her finger along the outside of the glass, collecting condensation. She held her finger out into the air, watched the water pool around her fingerprint in a bead, and watched the bead fall.

"My sister used to live in that place."

"How do you know she lived in my place?" he said.

"She lived on the top floor, right in the corner. Kind of hard to miss it," she said.

He craned his neck around, tried to make eye contact with her. Her eyes were evasive. He settled back into his chair.

"You miss her or something?" he said.

"Or something," she said.

"When'd she move out?" he said.

"She never moved out," she said. She took another, longer, sip of her drink before adding, "She died about a month ago."

"Oh, sorry," he said.

For the first time, he looked past her reflection to the outside, settled his eyes on a dancing plastic bag on the street and watched as passing cars catapulted it into the atmosphere, spinning and twirling.

"I lost my grandpa just a little bit ago," he said. "I know how you feel."

"Yeah? Did he jump off a fucking balcony too?" she said.

Gideon, who had just finished taking a sip of his pop, almost dropped the glass. He fumbled with it and spilled a bit on his jeans. He placed it back onto the table and pushed it close to the centre, then picked up a napkin and dabbed at his jeans for far too long, becoming lost in thought. What had the landlord told him when he thought the previous tenant might have a key? It wasn't possible, the landlord had said. Gideon understood why now. He kept dabbing away at his jeans, and the woman sat where she was, at times turning the glass around in her fingers, at times taking a sip, at times picking at the tape-cassette-shaped coaster.

"What was she like?" he said, breaking the silence.

He placed the napkin back on the table and slid it over beside his glass.

"She was…" she said, but her voice started to crack. She gathered herself, then continued, "Beautiful and sad."

"Why was she sad?" Gideon said.

"You don't know me," she said. "You don't know me to ask that. Don't ask that."

"Okay, then," he said. "How was she beautiful?"

This wasn't met with such defensiveness. Gideon thought perhaps it was nice for her to think about her sister. Nice but painful. He did the same with Grace, with his grandpa. Even dreamt about them. Their features, to him, were still clear, as though he was looking at a photograph of them. He hoped they'd be like that forever. Frozen in time, unchangeable.

"She had black hair, so black and full. Perfect brown skin. Big bold eyes. She was just beautiful, you know?"

When Gideon heard the description of the woman's sister, his heart pretty near stopped right then and there. The woman looked at him as though he was sick.

"You okay?" she said.

He nodded. He reached over and grabbed his glass of pop firmly. He took a sip and placed it back on the table.

"What was her name?" he said.

"Evelyn," she said.

She finished her beer, placed the glass back onto the coaster, pushed it to the other side of the table. She stood up.

"Look, I have to go," she said.

There was one lonely tear falling down her cheek, just like the bead of condensation that fell from her finger. He stood up too.

"She's not really gone, you know," he said.

She pushed hair behind her ear again, the same lock she had tucked behind her ear before. Her eyebrows scrunched together.

"What're you talking about?" she said.

He didn't answer at first. He picked up his drink and let an ice cube slip into his mouth. He chewed it thoughtfully. Finally, he said, "I mean, when you keep somebody in your heart, they don't ever die. Not really."

She wiped the tear away.

"Thanks," she said.

As Gideon walked home later, he still wasn't sure why he'd changed his mind about telling the woman about Evelyn. Maybe it was because she never would've believed him, might've told him to fuck off, stormed out of the pub, and he'd never see her again. And maybe it was because he wanted to see her again—not Evelyn, but the woman in the bar—despite her sunken eyes, despite her tangled hair, despite the hardship on her face. Maybe that was closest to the truth. In future days, he would search for her face along the crowded streets of downtown, not Alice's, not Evelyn's. In future days, on his walks, he would pass by the Yellow Dog Tavern to see if she was sitting there, staring out at nothing in particular.

Gideon woke up to a knock on the door. When he opened his eyes, he saw Evelyn lying on the floor in the same place he had seen her before. She was looking at the ceiling, the blank ceiling, and didn't turn her head when he stood up from the futon. There was another knock. He didn't move. He was afraid to. He didn't want her to run off again. Another knock.

"Gideon," said a voice through the door.

It was Alice. To his surprise, his heart kept a steady pace. His skin stayed dry. The world stayed still.

"I know you're there. It's almost midnight," Alice said.

He looked to the door, to the tiny circle of light coming from the peephole. She was there behind the door. She'd come to see him. He'd asked her to.

Another knock.

"Open up," Alice said.

He took a step toward the door but stopped. He turned his head back to Evelyn. She was still lying there, still staring at the ceiling, those beautiful big eyes wide open and transfixed by something; most certainly not the endless collection of tack holes in the drywall, most certainly not the white paint. He wished that he could see what she did. He saw for the first time how her skin shimmered with the evening light, as though a part of it. He took one careful step after another until he was right beside Evelyn, and farther away from the front door.

Another knock.

He got down onto his knees, placed his hands against the hardwood, and lowered himself to the floor. He turned onto his back, looked over at Evelyn. She didn't move. Not her head. Not her body. He heard a frustrated sigh from outside the front door. He lifted his head and looked at the shaft of light coming from the space between the door and the floor. He could see Alice's feet shifting this way and that. He knew her camouflage-patterned Converse shoes anywhere. After a few moments, they walked away. He listened as the sound of her footsteps trailed off down the hallway. He heard the elevator's shrill ding. He heard the doors rattle open. He heard the doors slide shut.

Gideon placed his hand over his chest. Still calm. He rested his head against the floor and turned toward Evelyn, her midnight-black hair, her dark olive skin, her saucer eyes, and then he looked away, toward the emptiness of the ceiling above, toward dreams of white nothingness. He let out a deep, cleansing sigh.

TWELVE

Alice still remembered the first time she'd been to the city. She was young, and her mother had taken her to Zellers. It was April and the store was busy as people prepared for Easter—shoppers at check-outs had carts full of chocolate bunnies with yellow and blue eyes and cheap pastel-coloured wicker Easter baskets filled with green plastic grass. Alice was entranced by all the stuff at the department store. She followed her mother around the store touching bikes, dolls, clothes, toys, and a million other things. She asked her mother to buy everything she touched, but each time her mother said no.

"We're not here to buy junk," her mother said. "We can't afford it."

"Everybody else is buying fun stuff!" Alice said.

At the checkout, her mother placed boring items on the conveyer belt and, one by one, they rolled up to the cashier—toilet paper and canned food and boxed food and toothpaste. Then a Cadbury cream egg, in its alluring purple and red shiny wrapping, caught Alice's eye. She wanted it so badly, but her mother would never buy it for her. She only bought cheap things. So Alice shoved it into her pocket and planned to eat it in the back seat on the way home. Upon leaving the store, Alice followed her mother through the parking lot and to their car but was stopped before she could climb into the back seat.

"What's that in your pocket?" her mother said.

"Nothing," Alice said.

She tried to hide the bulge by shoving her hand into her pocket, but it was too late. Her mother pushed Alice's hand out of the way, reached into the pocket, and pulled out the egg. She looked like she could've crushed it in her hand she was so mad, but instead gave Alice a sharp slap on the bum.

"I've never been more disappointed in you, Alice," her mother said.

"I'm sorry!" Alice said through tears.

Her mother grabbed Alice by the arm, dragged her back inside the department store, and right to the front of the busy checkout line they'd just left, much to the displeasure of impatient Easter shoppers. Her mother made Alice hand the cashier the Cadbury cream egg.

"I took this. I'm sorry," Alice said.

"What a shock," the cashier said as he took the egg with an exaggerated sigh.

Alice noticed her mother's jaws were clenched as she rummaged through her change purse and handed the cashier money.

"Well, at least you had the good sense to bring it back. Most of you only return stuff when you're caught," he said, then turned to Alice and handed her the egg.

"Here you go, kid. Enjoy."

The Cadbury cream egg was resting in her palm, glittering in the bright store lights. She looked at her mom, then the cashier, and finally handed the egg back.

"No thanks," she said.

JUMPER

IN HER BASEMENT APARTMENT, snuggled between Kathy and Jayne, Alice used the light of her cell phone to study the worn photograph of her and her girls. Grace was on the far left of the line, smiling so hard that her eyes nearly disappeared, taken over as they were by her cheeks. Next to Grace, Jayne, leaning forward on her elbows, her fingers locked together tightly, her beautiful long black hair tossed up in the air, whipping around like a flag, and a cute little half smile that made it look like she was winking at the camera. Kathy was next in the line, always slightly understated, always seeming a bit older than her years, her eyes kind of slanted down toward the sides of her face like sideways teardrops, her closed-mouthed smile creating subtle dimples on each cheek, the right cheek carrying a deeper dimple than the left, and her chin resting on her right fist. Then there was Alice, her black hair pushed back behind her ears, her eyes looking directly into the camera, directly at the photographer, her then-boyfriend Ryan.

Alice turned the phone's camera on so that she could see herself, and moved the phone beside the photograph so there was a real-time image of her face added to the family portrait. She looked back and forth, from Alice then to Alice now, and wished she'd known then what she knew now. The pain then seemed a pittance. She would gladly trade it for what she felt currently. Give me the beatings, she thought. Give me the bruises and the clothing to cover them up. Give me the shame and give me the meekness.

Give me all of it, she thought, just give me Grace. Please, God, just give me Grace. She looked at her eyes in the photograph, the deception in them.

"Smile, Alice," Ryan had said. "Just try to smile."

She tried. She really did. She looked at her girls to elicit a smile. Tried to ignore Ryan crouching behind the camera. But he was right there.

"Don't ruin the picture," he said.

She managed to push the corners of her mouth upward. She was afraid if she didn't he would make her pay for it later. She saw his knuckles on either side of the camera. She could almost feel them against her jaw, her stomach, her arms.

"Get your hair out of the way. It's covering your face," he said.

With shaking fingers, she did. She pushed her hair behind her ears. Looked at her girls again. She didn't want them dealing with her getting beaten again, running off to the bathroom, locking themselves inside until he left to cool off.

"Look at the camera. Look at me, damn it," he said.

She did. She looked through the lens, right at him.

"Fine. That's fine," he said with the same tone he used so often, stark and disappointed, the one that made her know she was going to get it later. She'd ruined it. She'd ruined it again. If she could go back to that moment, she would have smiled so big and so hard.

Alice re-examined the photograph by the light of her cell phone. She looked to the field behind them that stretched far into the horizon, where a line of trees in the distance looked like a strip of Velcro holding up a perfect blue felt sky; to the tire swing just visible on the right side of the picture that allowed her to reach into the heavens and watch the girls play amidst the long grass; to Grace, who would be young forever, forever in the field, filled with an immeasurable joy; then at Kathy and Jayne, who were still with her, who would age, who would find joy, who would suffer, who would laugh, who would cry. In that moment, Alice wondered where she would want those things to happen. In the city everything was close but felt as far away as the tree line on the horizon behind her trailer. It was loud and cold and frightening. She thought back on her time there, and on how it had gone so terribly wrong.

Days earlier she had left the second-floor bathroom on her way to the basement, where she and the girls had been staying. Alice had spent so much time in the claw-foot tub since moving to the city that she might as well have had permanent prune hands and toes. It was the only place in the entire city, in that small bathroom with cracked powder-blue walls and scratched linoleum flooring, that she was able to trick her body into feeling relaxed. When she had navigated her way down the stairs, carefully avoiding the protruding staples on the last few steps where the paper-thin carpet was coming up, she walked past the laundry room and into her makeshift apartment.

Krista had set up a twin-sized mattress in the middle of the room, had moved her son's hockey equipment into the laundry room to make the space. The smell of sweaty hockey equipment still hung in the air, though, even weeks after it had been removed. Scented candles just made it seem like the equipment was burning. There was a bathroom down there, but the water was usually yellow and the showerhead was broken and sprayed water all over the place. Alice and the girls didn't use it much, except to pee in the middle of the night. Alice could never tell if the girls had flushed, on account of the basement water's colour. And the fluorescent bulbs were dim, and the soul-sucking flickering light gave Alice a constant headache. Her cousin had set up a small television set near the foot of the bed, and that's often where the girls were. That's where they were when Alice entered the room.

They looked like pieces of furniture in that depressing basement apartment. Their eyes were vacantly taking in an episode of Power Rangers for whatever damn reason. That wasn't a typical show for them. Alice felt her heart sink.

"Darlings," she said, "do you want to go play outside?"

She surprised herself when she said that. The girls hadn't been outside for several days by this point. The last time they'd been outside, out in front of the house, Alice had given them clear instructions on where they could go: no farther than the white picket fence to the right, four houses down, and the fire hydrant to the left, three houses down. Letting them go out there at all was an enormous step Alice had taken. She wasn't comfortable letting them play outside back home on the rez, where cars passed by infrequently. In the city, outside their new home, speed bumps had been created by the city due to the frequent, fast, and oblivious traffic. Alice had been watching them from the front step, and, when Jayne wandered onto the boulevard from the sidewalk, that was that. The girls were called over and sent down to the basement. Having them watch television was far safer than allowing them near a busy street.

Jayne jumped up as though she'd received an electrical shock. She raced past Alice and up the stairs. Kathy didn't get up at first. She looked up to her mother inquisitively.

"Really?" she said.

Alice nodded. "Yes, really."

Kathy stood up, and Alice walked with her up the stairs, where Jayne was waiting by the side door.

"Can we go out front?" Jayne said.

She had a bigger smile on her face than Alice had ever seen.

"No," Alice said. "You can play in the back yard."

"But it's all muddy back there. There's no grass," Kathy said.

"There's hardly any grass back home either," Alice said.

"There's only grass back home in the field," Kathy said.

"Please, Mommy?" Jayne said.

"There's no grass in the driveway back home, and you girls like playing there just fine," Alice said.

Kathy gave up. She took Jayne's hand as Alice opened the door. The girls walked outside.

"Come on, Jayne, it's better than nothing," Kathy said.

Alice followed behind her girls as they walked to the back yard, right to the middle, and looked around as though lost. Alice surveyed the area. She hadn't been out there much. Neither had the girls. But Kathy was right. It was almost all dirt back there. Even the box garden near the back of the yard sat unattended, full not with vegetables or plants but rather with bad soil and weeds. She watched Jayne race over to one of the rare clumps of grass and playfully flick at the blades. Kathy aimlessly wandered around the yard as Jayne went from clump of grass to clump of grass. Eventually, Jayne had visited all the clumps and began to wander around with Kathy. The two of them held hands and simply walked from one end to the other. Alice watched all of this, and she couldn't help but notice how their eyes, their shoulders, began to look the same as when she had found them in front of the television set.

"There are toys in the garage, I think," Alice called out.

The girls ignored her. They walked over to the box garden and sat on its edge. Jayne's exuberance was gone. They weakly held hands and stared at the dirt.

"Why aren't you girls playing?" Alice said.

"There's nothing to do," Kathy said.

"You didn't look in the garage," Alice said.

Kathy shook her head. "I've been in there before, Mom. There are sand toys in there. There is dirt out here."

"Well, why don't you play hide-and-seek then?" Alice said.

Alice saw Jayne start to get up, but Kathy squeezed Jayne's hand and held her back.

"There's nowhere to hide, Mom," Kathy said.

Alice looked around at the back yard. Kathy was right again. There was nowhere to hide. She sighed.

"Okay, you can go out front," Alice said.

Neither girl got up.

"That's okay," Kathy said.

Alice walked over to her girls. She sat down at the edge of the box garden and put her arm around both of them. Back home the girls had shown signs of missing their little sister, whether they realized it or not. They hadn't played as hard or as frequently, hadn't laughed as often, hadn't seemed to enjoy things like they used to. In the city, however, they seemed to get more depressed and lonely with each passing day. And it wasn't just that Grace wasn't there. Gideon wasn't either. The only times when the girls seemed normal were the times they'd spent with him. Alice had realized this earlier. She'd even texted him recently, hoping that he'd have the time to visit her. He hadn't texted her back. She imagined how he must have felt when he came by her house to find they were gone. She didn't blame him for not texting her. She wouldn't have either.

She often thought back to something Gideon had said just weeks after Grace died, when she had floated the idea, for the first time, of leaving the rez, even though back then it was something she'd said out of emotion, not intent. "You know," he'd said, "my grandpa always says that you can't run away from memories and emotions and shit. They're faster than you could ever be." She'd told him to fuck off at the time, but now that she'd left, now that she'd been gone for a few weeks, she saw that he'd been right. The city had only made things worse. Grace was everywhere, even though she was nowhere. She'd followed them there, to the dingy and depressing apartment, to the rush of it all, to the crushing closeness. The memories had come, small ones and big ones, all of them suffocating, and just as frequently as back home. So, going to the city was no escape. Where was there an escape? When would she be free from the pain? She squeezed her daughters hard, leaned over and kissed them on their foreheads.

"I love you both so much," she said.

"I love you, too," Kathy said.

"I love you, Mommy," Jayne said.

Alice stood up.

"You can play out here for as long as you want, okay?" Alice said.

"Where are you going?" Kathy said.

"Just for a walk," Alice said.

She made her way to the side of the house and then turned around. She took another, long look at her girls. They were beautiful, they really were. Everything good about her was in them.

She didn't have any real destination. She ambled through the alleyways and avenues of the city in a vain attempt to get lost from everything, from Grace, from herself. Walks in the city weren't the same as walks on the rez—that much was clear and unsurprising. It was so loud in the city, deafening really, and her eyes rested not against the vastness of the rez and the quiet of its seclusion, but rather against the concrete and steel of the city, cold and austere. Eventually she arrived at a bridge that arched over a railway yard and made her way up, at times travelling faster than the crowd of cars to her left because traffic was backed up considerably.

At the top of the bridge she was hit with a gust of wind and stopped to feel the air push against her body. When the breeze had died down, she looked out across the railway yard, up to the steel arches that cut the daytime sky into pieces, and for a moment she was not lost, but rather felt calm move through her body. The bitter stench of the city washed away along with its distractions. Gone was the rush of it all, the busyness. Alice looked down, where the train cars looked like coffins, the railway tracks like a confused roadmap, and in that view she was sure she'd found her destination.

She turned away for a moment and scanned the annoyed and angry faces in the bumper-to-bumper traffic on the bridge, the fists punching steering wheels, the mouths lipping profanities, the scrunched foreheads, and then her eyes met with a man's. She found her gaze frozen there, locked to him, and it was as if his gaze was locked to hers as well. It seemed to her that he intended to say something. A ridiculous idea came to her. Perhaps this man was the angel she'd been looking for, she'd been thinking about, ever since Grace's death. She made a bargain. If he said something to her, she wouldn't jump. She would consider his words a sign that there was another way to escape Grace's memory.

He opened his lips, and she watched as they showed the man's hesitancy, the back and forth that was going on in his mind. They opened then shut, opened then shut. Then, traffic began to lurch forward, and the man moved forward with it. She listened for his words, waited, hoped for them to come to her, above the murmuring engines, above the bleating horns, above all the frenzied noise of rush hour in the city, but he didn't say anything. She watched as his car crested the hill and descended into another part of the city, away from her.

So be it.

She sighed deeply, then looked skyward. She might have mouthed a prayer, offering words to splash against the overhead grey canvas but didn't want to give the satisfaction, not to God, and certainly not to a supposed angel. So, empty-minded, she turned back toward the side of the bridge, walked forward slowly, and lifted herself up onto the ledge. There, she stood as straight as could be, certain she had never been quite as high. She stretched her arms out as wide as they could go and began to sway back and forth like the long grass in the field behind her trailer. Jump, please jump, she thought, but her legs wouldn't move. She tilted her head backwards, stared into the sky. Please, you want this. Don't you want this? She heard cars stop behind her, doors open then shut, footsteps gathering around the place she stood.

"Come on, lady."

"Get down from there."

"Talk to me. I'm right here."

She looked around. There were four or five people just below her, looking up to her, pleading to her, reaching for her. There were four or five people, but not the man she had seen, and no angel. But why did she keep thinking about it? Was that why she had come? Not to end her life, as she thought, but rather to test something her girls had told her? Was she still so desperate to believe it? She turned away from the small crowd that had gathered, shaking her head, back to the sky, and stood up there for a long time, lost in thought. Then, eventually, she had one final thought: the angel will come, or I will go to my Grace. Either way, there was peace.

Her legs obeyed, and she stepped forward. She heard shouting behind her, desperate pleas, felt wind rushing against her skin. And it was in that moment, when she was sure it was too late, that she knew she didn't want to die. It was the way her body reacted as she started to lose her balance, how she whipped her arms back and forth like an injured bird as she tried desperately to steady herself. If you had seen this from below, where the railway tracks were, you would have seen her body embossed against the wide and uniformly grey sky, her arms flapping up and down. And you might have thought that she looked as though she were making snow angels in a vast and open field. You might also have been surprised to see, in the following moment, her body suddenly straighten and calm, as though one of the people behind her had caught her in time. But nobody had touched her. Somehow, some way, she had found her balance.

Alice placed her thumb on the photograph so that it covered Grace's face, so it was just Jayne, Kathy, and Alice. She scanned the photograph, removed her thumb, and scanned it again. She had done this from time to time since the girls had fallen asleep, testing how it felt with Grace not there, how it felt with her beside her sisters and her mother. It felt the same, though. Even with Grace's face covered, she was there. She looked at her girls, resting quietly on either side of her. There was no doubt. She was worse, they were worse, where they were. Moving to the city hadn't removed Grace from their life, and it had taken much more from them. Alice couldn't believe, either, that she had considered taking herself from her girls' lives, too. What would they have left? No. They belonged together where Grace would always be, and with her the good memories and with her the bad memories.

Still holding the photograph, she shifted the phone around in her hands and found Gideon's number. She'd gone to see him after he'd eventually texted back, but he didn't answer the door, or wasn't there. But she knew he was in the city too. Why had he come to the city? Was he having the same sort of troubles she was having? She hoped he would respond. She hoped he would be there for her still, even though she didn't feel as though she deserved it.

She sent him a text that read: "I want to go home."

Alice placed her phone and the photograph on the nightstand beside the bed. She lay back down, nestled between Jayne and Kathy. Carefully, trying not to wake them, she slipped one arm beneath Jayne and her other arm beneath Kathy, and gathered them both close to her body. They felt warm and safe, and they'd been away from her arms for too long. She fell asleep that night listening to a collision of nighttime sounds; the white-noise hum of the refrigerator, the on-again-off-again low rumble of the furnace, and, most of all, the calm breaths of her daughters. She slept so well that she didn't hear a text notification that arrived deep in the night. She wouldn't read it until the morning. It was a message from Gideon.

"I'll take you there."

THIRTEEN

Sometimes all you could hear at Alice's place was Grace's footsteps as she raced from one place to the next. She ran flat-footed, and the soles of her feet slapped against the floor like applause. It was one of the reasons why, in the trailer, she wasn't the best hide-and-seek player. When Kathy or Jayne closed their eyes and counted to 10, they could hear exactly where Grace was headed. Not only that, but, as Kathy or Jayne looked for her, she would almost always call out "I'm here!" because, to her, the best thing about hide-and-seek was being found. The bigger girls, they'd pretend to look for her to amuse her, often right up until Grace notified them of exactly where she was. When they found her, Grace would cry out in delight and stuff her fingers into her mouth excitedly. Then, they'd do it all over again. The only time she stayed hidden was when Kathy would hide with her. Kathy would carry Grace around the trailer to avoid the announcement of her clumsy and loud footsteps, take her somewhere and put Grace on her lap and shush her. Then it would take Jayne a bit longer to find them.

In the field, of course, things were different. Grace's footsteps were the same, but they were silent against the soil. And when she called out 'I'm here!' it didn't matter, because Grace was so small and the grass was so high that it still took Kathy and Jayne forever to find her. Out in the field, Grace was the best hider, despite herself.

These days, Kathy and Jayne still play hide-and-seek. Not in the trailer, mind you. They never play there. But when they're allowed to go out into the field, they play like they used to. Kathy and Jayne, they never hide from each other, though. They count to 10 together and go off, hand in hand, to search through the long grass for Grace.

STONY MOUNTAIN SERENADE

A LICE SAT NERVOUSLY. She stared at her own reflection in the thick glass in front of her, the seat on the other side empty and waiting, and carefully inspected her face. She tried her best not to care but did wonder, despite herself, what Ryan would think of her appearance. She was nothing like before. She'd felt alive, and her face reflected that vibrancy. She had felt so much prettier then, and she must have been. Otherwise, Ryan would've had nothing to do with her. He was that kind of guy back then. He was probably still that kind of guy. But why did she care what he thought, damn it? Why were her palms so sweaty? Why was her heartbeat so quick?

In the reflection she saw every tired, deep line on her face. She thought of when they first met and how she looked now after everything that had happened, the hurricane that was their relationship, the relief of seeing him gone, and, finally, the pain of losing Grace. She looked away, down to her hands, her fingers clasped desperately, shaking and sweaty and cold. She worried about holding the telephone receiver, if she'd be able to keep her hands still when he arrived. Perhaps it was better to think about that than what he would think about seeing her. But, God, why did she have to be so unsettled in the first place? He always did this to her. He always broke her down. He always changed her.

She had felt brave walking into Stony Mountain Penitentiary. She had walked in confidently, with her chest puffed out and proud, her chin high. It had been a good day, and good days were rare. Alice cherished days like today. Gideon had come by in the morning to pick Kathy, Jayne, and her up. The girls were happy to see him. It had been too long since they'd spent time with him. She regretted leaving the rez like she had, even though, at the time, it felt necessary. She saw what it had done to the girls. They were lonely and empty from the loss of Grace, and then she'd moved them away from their surrogate uncle. She wondered what it had done to Gideon, too. But he'd loaded up the truck in good spirits, and they left. It felt good when the city was in the rear-view mirror, like she could breathe again.

The farther they went, the smaller the city got, and soon the penitentiary loomed on the horizon. Despite everything that had happened with Ryan, she'd always felt drawn there, ever since he'd been convicted. Just like each time he hit her and she wanted to leave, but stayed. It was different this time. She wanted to see him of her own volition. She knew she had words for him, just not what those words were. But she was sure they'd come in their own time, they would be said, and he would hear them. She had trusted in that until she'd sat down to wait for him. Then the trust faded.

She unclasped her fingers and rested her hands, palms up, on the desk in front of her. She looked at them carefully, inspecting the lines on her palms as though they were a roadmap, as though she were lost somewhere. Her hands—they always got shaky and cold when she was scared or nervous. For no particular reason, Alice thought of when she'd been afraid to get onto the plane to Anchorage to visit relatives. She'd never flown before. Ryan had seen her hands clasping the sides of her seat and had sung a song he wrote for her—he always sang that song to calm her. She heard his voice:

Walk on down the side of the road,
Walk until I see my soul.

But I can't stand
The sight of my life tonight.

She was never sure if it was the lyrics or his voice that calmed her. All she knew was that later, when Ryan started to scare her, when Ryan made her nervous, there was no song any more, and so there was no calm.

A knock against the glass brought Alice back. She looked up to see him sitting down. She noticed immediately how the blue prison jumpsuit brought out his eyes. She tried hard not to look at them. It was an odd feeling—being drawn to them but feeling sick to her stomach at the same time. It was always in the eyes. Always, after he had beat on her and had returned from one of his walks, he would talk sweet to her, strike her with those eyes, and she'd take him back, forgive him. And hate herself a little more. He pointed to the telephone receiver at her side. She nodded and fumbled with it just as she had feared. Her fingers felt as though she'd been out in the cold. She held it to her ear.

The two of them sat with the thick pane of glass between them and didn't say anything for a long time. Alice closed her eyes. It was like the first time they'd spoken on the phone before they started dating, when they didn't say anything for the longest time, just listened to each other's nervous breaths. They spoke in breaths now, and their breathing said enough. Her breath was quick and quivering. She didn't want it to be because she didn't want him to know how she felt, or that she felt anything at all. She listened to his breath carefully and tried to hear how he felt. His breath was steady, measured, and it disappointed her. She opened her eyes.

"I thought you didn't want to talk to me again," he said.

"I didn't," she said. "I don't."

He didn't look away from her, nor did he blink. How could he not blink? Alice took a deep breath that didn't calm her. Even through the murky glass his eyes were clear blue. She tore her eyes away from his and looked at a deep bruise on his forearm.

"What's that from?" she said.

"Don't mind it," he said. "Don't worry."

"I'm not worried," she said.

He rubbed the bruise, then crossed his arms to cover it. The phone receiver rested between his shoulder and ear.

"It gets rough in here," he said.

She scanned the rest of his body. She didn't see any other bruises. She was surprised that this disappointed her.

"Do you have lots of those?" she said.

"Some," he said.

She involuntarily rubbed her own skin—her cheek, her neck. There were no bruises for her to cover any more. She looked him in the eyes again.

"How does it feel when you get hurt?" she said.

Ryan shifted in his seat, let out a sigh, and looked away. He didn't have to answer her; she knew damn well how it felt and she could only hope that he knew then how she'd felt when he'd put his hands on her. The way she was then, meek and small and damaged, is how he looked now. She started to say something but stopped herself. She wanted to see the bruises he had been given, but it was not like her to want something like that.

"Are you afraid in there?" she said.

"Sometimes," he said.

He sat up straight. He looked at the desk in front of him. There was nothing on the desk. She inspected his face. There were large bags under his eyes and deep lines like cracks on a windshield. He looked older than he had been before he was arrested. He looked older than he should have. She looked closer. There were tiny cuts on his lips, but not because his lips were chapped.

"What's wrong with your lips?" she said.

He shook his head.

"Nothing," he said.

"Nothing?" she said.

He took a deep breath. She saw his chest rise and fall.

"I was eating glass," he said quietly, perhaps hoping she wouldn't hear him.

"You what? Why would you do that?" she said.

He didn't answer.

"Ryan, why would you do that?"

He slumped forward on his arms and his head dropped. She hadn't seen him like this before. She sat up a bit straighter.

He spoke without lifting his head. "You know, when I was younger, my dad used to lock me in his closet. He did worse stuff, I guess, but I hated being in that fucking closet. I think I'm, like, claustrophobic or something. I always felt like I was getting crushed in there."

Alice nodded. This was news to her. Ryan had never talked about his childhood. He never really opened up about anything.

"Being in that cell reminds me of being in my dad's closet. I need to get out of here, but there isn't any getting out. Not for a while."

He lifted his head up. He rubbed at his lips. He chuckled.

"I heard that if I started bleeding inside they'd bring me to the hospital, so I ate a fucking light bulb. Figured it would get me out of here for a bit," he said.

"Ryan," she said.

He chuckled harder. He laughed without smiling.

"I didn't get anywhere though. Tried it a few times. Didn't bleed once where I needed to."

Alice turned away because she didn't want him to see her face, didn't want him to know she felt bad for him. She wished she didn't care at all. She wanted him to think she was strong and resilient, that she was getting on fine without him, that he wasn't needed, not by the girls, and not by her. But then her hand, which had settled down, began to shake. Her breathing was short, and she began to tremble. She held the receiver away from her mouth so he couldn't hear it.

"Do the girls ever ask about me?" he said.

She shook her head without looking at him.

"No," she said, "they don't."

The silence returned. Alice closed her eyes. She remembered the silence after he would return from one of his walks, the silence after he told her he was sorry, after he kissed her bruises. He used to wait for her forgiveness, and she always forgave him, and maybe she meant it. Maybe she'd meant it each time. She was never sure what she was more afraid of: being with him, or alone.

"I have that picture of you and the girls still," he said. "The one where you're all in the field."

She nodded. She was still hiding her face and she needed to calm herself.

"I have it tacked up on my wall. It's the only good thing in my cell, that picture on my wall," he said.

"That's nice. That's a nice picture," she said.

"Everybody looks so happy," he said. "When I look at that picture, I can just see everything happening right then. It was so windy. The girls' hair all whipping around in the wind. It was so fucking windy. You looked happy too," he said.

Alice looked at him and saw that he was looking right at her with those perfect blue eyes.

"We weren't happy," she said.

"Sure we were," he said. "Sure you were."

Alice shook her head.

"Do you remember what happened before that picture? Right before that picture?" she said.

He shook his head.

"No, I don't remember," he said.

"Of course you don't," she said.

There was another silence. Alice closed her eyes. She thought of when the RCMP drove away with Ryan in the back seat. She had wanted silence for a long time—the silence in the breeze, in the endless field of grass behind her house, within the walls of her trailer. She opened her eyes. She had done the same thing with that picture; pretended it was something other than what it was. She couldn't really blame him for doing the same.

"I miss Grace, you know," he said.

She looked away. Her hand started to shake even more. Her chest felt hot. She felt like slamming the receiver against the wall.

"What about the other girls?" she said.

"What do you mean?" he said.

"You never see them. They may as well all be dead. Kathy, Jayne, and Grace. Do you miss all of them?" she said.

"Of course I miss all of them. I miss you too," he said.

"Don't tell me you miss me," she said.

This time, she couldn't hide her shaking hand from him. She was looking at the floor, at her camouflage Converse sneakers, when she heard the first notes of the song, his song. She kept looking at her sneakers when she heard his voice.

Walk on down the side of the road,
Walk until I see my soul.
But I can't stand
The sight of my life tonight.
Walk on down the side of the road,
All these memories getting old,
And I guess that
All I have is what I had.

She looked up suddenly. She looked right at him.

"Walk on down…"

"I don't want you to sing to me. You can't sing to me anymore."

When she said those words, her hand stopped shaking and her breath evened out. Perhaps that's what she had wanted to say to him all along.

She started to stand, but Ryan called out, "Alice, wait."

"What?" she said.

There was silence. She kept her eyes trained on him, and she held his gaze. She'd seen this look before, after his walks, each time he had asked her to forgive him, each time he had waited for an answer.

"I'm sorry. I'm so sorry for everything," he said.

She knew what she'd said too many times before. She nodded her head and hung up the receiver.

"I know you are," she mouthed.

She walked away.

FOURTEEN

Morgan got off the 17, relieved to be alone when the bus pulled away from the curb. She always felt the same way at the end of bus rides. Why did she feel lonelier when she was around people than when she was actually alone? She could only reason that the memories kept her better company, as painful as they were.

She crossed the street toward Central Park and once inside surveyed the scenery as though there might be something different to see. The splash pad to the right was shut down and unoccupied. She'd rarely seen the water turned on or children playing in it, or children playing anywhere else in the park for that matter. She always chose the right time for her visits—the fewer people the better. She followed the cement pathway through the park, walking between the splash pad and the field with its cheap artificial turf, the kind of green shit she remembered stapled to the roof of her adopted father's nativity scene. It made her sick to look at it. When she finally made it across the park and hopped over the black wrought iron fence, she was once again relieved.

And then she stood there, in the middle of the sidewalk, looking up to the top floor of an apartment building on Cumberland, her eyes fixed on an empty balcony, her mind imagining something there. A figure in the shadows, somebody with their eyes fixed back on her.

After she'd been standing there for a few minutes, she felt a gentle tap on her shoulder and turned around to see a familiar face: the man she'd met briefly at the Yellow Dog Tavern. He smiled at her but seemed unsure of what to say. They looked at each other a moment and then together looked up to the empty balcony.

"I think I can see her sometimes," Morgan said. "Evelyn."

"Yeah," the man said. "That happens when you miss somebody a lot."

They were quiet for a time, and in the silence Morgan wondered why he had stopped to talk to her. She'd wondered the same thing the last time she'd seen him. She would've thought he was stalking her if she wasn't in front of his own apartment building. Still, she didn't want him to leave. He wasn't like one of the passengers on her bus. He was different.

"My name's Morgan," she said.

"Gideon," he said.

"It's nice to meet you," she said. "Again."

"You too, again."

She heard squeaking from the splash pad. She recognized the sound. Somebody had sat down on one of the flower-petal seats and was spinning around. She'd stood in this place so often that she knew all the sounds. It was an odd place to know best.

"You know, if you keep lookin' up, you're gonna miss somethin' right in front of you," Gideon said.

She nodded her head, sighed. How many nights had she stood there? How many times had she pictured her sister on the balcony, then climbing over the side, then falling to the sidewalk below? But still she couldn't, or perhaps wouldn't, look away.

SKETCHES

ALICE ALWAYS THOUGHT that if she did go and see Ryan she would leave in tears, angry and devastated, or feel like she had left a piece of herself behind, that he had taken something from her again. She never thought she would leave feeling more whole than she had in a long time. Yet there she was, walking away from the jail with a smile. She wasn't beaming, mind you, but it was good enough. And, at first, when she saw Gideon's truck in the parking lot, she smiled a little bigger, because, if you had told her a few days ago that she would be in a truck with him heading home, she would have thought you were crazy.

But as Alice got closer she noticed that Gideon's face was slumped downward and didn't hold the levity hers did. So, as she placed her hand on the passenger-side door handle, her own smile washed away. She didn't blame him for it, though. Over the years he'd been there for her, to hold an ice pack on the places where Ryan had done the most damage, to dress her wounds, to hold her close against his body to let her know she was safe. And now there she was, leaving from a visit with Ryan, and looking glad about it. She got in the truck.

"So," he said, sounding pissed.

She looked back at the girls to avoid responding. She didn't like how he'd asked but also didn't know what she could say. There was nothing that would've made him feel better about it anyway. Kathy was reading. She didn't really do anything else lately, except when she was playing with Jayne. Jayne was busy colouring in one of her Disney princess colouring books. Alice craned her neck to get a closer look.

"Oh, Snow White," she said to Jayne.

"You gonna tell me what happened in there or what?" Gideon said.

Alice turned back toward the front and looked at Gideon.

"Not if you've already made up your mind about it before I even say anything," Alice said.

"Al," he said, "there's only one way it goes with him."

"Well, it went fine anyway," she said.

Gideon shook his head.

"That's all I get?" he said. "Fine?"

"It's private," she said.

He exhaled aggressively through his nose, like a bull, and put the truck into drive. The truck began to move and then stopped abruptly, causing everybody to lurch forward then resettle. He put it back into park.

"After all we've gone through, you're gonna tell me that something's private?" he shout-whispered in an attempt to shield the girls from knowing they were fighting.

Alice looked out the passenger side window. She scanned the cars in the parking lot, looked back at the jail, and then turned back to Gideon.

"I'm sorry, Gideon," Alice said. "But *we* didn't go through it, *I* did. You were there for me, and I'm thankful, but there's more to Ryan and me than bruises. There's more than you could ever understand, and I don't think I need to explain that to you."

"I think you should. I think you owe me at least that," Gideon said.

Alice put her hand on Gideon's.

"I owe you a lot, I know that, but I don't owe you this. This is between Ryan and me and nobody else," Alice said.

Gideon moved his hand away.

"What about the girls?" Gideon said.

"That's their father, Gideon. One day, it's something I'll have to tell them about. This is my family," Alice said.

"So what am I then?" Gideon said.

Alice hesitated. She'd never thought about it before. If she was honest about it to herself, Gideon seemed as much a part of her family as Olive or Sara. Hell, the girls even called him uncle. But she didn't want to share anything about Ryan with him, and she never had. She didn't understand why, but it was what it was.

"I see," Gideon said. "I get it."

"Gideon," Alice said.

He put the truck into drive.

"I'm not staying, you know. I'm just dropping you off," he said.

"Okay," she said. "Okay. I know."

He pushed his foot against the gas pedal, and the truck pulled away from the parking spot. Soon, Stony Mountain Penitentiary was in the rear-view mirror. When the truck pulled onto the highway, Alice turned back to her girls and figured that they'd been listening to her and Gideon. They'd stopped what they were doing and were looking out their respective windows.

"Kathy," she said. "Honey, why don't you keep reading."

Kathy turned away from the window. She picked the book up from her lap, curled her legs up onto her seat, and settled back into reading.

"Jayne," Alice said, "why don't you draw a picture for Mommy?"

Jayne looked away from the window. She nodded at Alice. She closed her colouring book and very neatly slid it into a cloth bag at her feet. She pulled out a sketch pad and flipped through page upon page of beautiful pictures, mostly of rainbows and castles and princesses, until she found a blank white sheet. She took out a plastic container of pencil crayons. She opened the lid, thoughtfully fingered through a variety of colours, but didn't take one out.

"What's wrong?" Alice said.

"I can't think of anything to draw," Jayne said.

"You'll think of something," Alice said.

Alice turned around. She looked at Gideon for a long while, waiting, hoping for him to look in her direction. He didn't. She spent the next hour of the drive glancing over at him curiously. He was always the one doing the talking, and now there was nothing. She thought back over the past year. For so long after Grace died, he'd come by her house and sat with her, talked to her, and she had said almost nothing in return. She wondered if he'd felt then how she felt now, and if so, she understood, in some way, how hard it must've been for him to be around her. Yet, he still came, almost every day. For the first time, she wondered if she was right to not tell him about her visit with Ryan. Did he deserve to know? What did he deserve?

Eventually she gave up trying to get his attention and resigned herself to staring out the passenger-side window as he looked resolutely ahead. There was nothing but trees and open road for her to see. In the fall the drive was beautiful, the trees golden and majestic, the grass beside the highway glittering like burning embers. This time of year, however, everything was green, and it reminded her of the neatly manicured lawns of the city, which was nowhere she wanted to be. She realized how much she preferred dead grass and bad land.

Eventually the quiet became unbearable, and Alice decided to change the one thing she could. She leaned forward to turn on the radio. There was static at first, which wasn't much of a surprise. Where they were, there wasn't good reception, not for cell phones and not for the radio. She flipped through FM stations, stopped every once in a while when she heard a hint of anything through the static, and finally found a pop radio station. She leaned back in the passenger seat and returned to staring out her window, serenaded now by Miley Cyrus. Almost instantly, Gideon let out an expressive groan.

"What?" Alice said.

"I hate this music," he said. "All sounds the same, you know. Even the women and the men, shit, can't tell them apart. All singing to the same beat, in the same key. Can't stand it."

He leaned over, turned off the radio.

"You sound like your grandpa, you know," Alice said.

Gideon shook his head. He turned the radio back on.

"What do you know about my grandpa?" he said.

Miley crooning over "We Can't Stop" nearly drowned him out, but Alice heard him.

"I know lots about him," she said.

"Yeah, you musta really cared about him," he said.

Alice reached over, turned the radio off.

"I did care about him," she said. "I do care."

"Why weren't you at his wake then? People who didn't even know him too good still showed up, even if it was for the food or whatever. They were still there."

"I..."

"And there I was starin' out the window and waitin' on you like some jackass," he said. "Like a god-damn dog."

"I was in the city. I couldn't come," she said, but corrected herself, because the distance wasn't why. "I couldn't go back."

"And just how far do you think I woulda come back for Grace, huh?" he said but didn't wait for Alice to respond. "I woulda went all the way around the world for Grace, for you and the girls. I woulda went all the way around the world twice."

Alice's knee-jerk reaction was to open her mouth and shoot something back, but there were no words to say. He was right. She'd heard from Olive that his grandpa had died. She'd almost gone back, she knew she should've, but she couldn't bring herself to go. Alice turned away, back to the passenger-side window and, in the silence, wiped a tear away from her cheek.

Half an hour later, Gideon's truck pulled up beside the barricade of stones Alice had constructed. Alice and Gideon sat in a familiar silence for a minute, as though they were both waiting for something that wasn't coming. Finally, Gideon opened the driver's-side door and stepped outside. Alice followed suit, and the girls, freed, rushed out of the passenger side of the truck. First Kathy, who shoved her way past Jayne, then Jayne, who gave Kathy a little kick in the pants on her way out. Kathy ran off down the driveway toward the front of the house. She picked up a ball, bounced it, and threw it into the old plastic basketball hoop. Jayne tugged at Alice's arm.

"What, my darling?" Alice said. "Go play."

Jayne handed her a folded-up piece of paper, then, quick as lightning, ran toward Kathy. She stole the ball from her sister and dunked it into the hoop. Kathy shouted at her, "Hey you little punk!"

Gideon walked around the front of the truck and met Alice near the passenger side door. He leaned up against the hood. Alice, cautiously, leaned against him, the paper Jayne had given her still in her hand. For a moment, she closed her eyes. She recalled the times when he would come into her bed and cuddle up beside her. He always knew just when she needed it, and he never tried to do anything else. He was always a gentleman. She put her head against his shoulder. He didn't move away.

"I'm sorry," she whispered.

Gideon took a deep breath. She wondered what he was thinking. He always just used to tell her his thoughts, whether she wanted to know them or not. She wanted that now. But things weren't the same. Maybe they wouldn't ever be.

"You know, all that matters to me is that you're here and he's not," she said. "Nothing else matters."

She leaned in closer, turned to him, put her arm around his waist. He put his hand on her forearm, held it there. She could feel him squeeze her arm slightly. Then he gently removed her arm from his waist.

"I met somebody back in the city," he said.

He stuck his hands into his jeans, looked at Alice, who stood there motionless, speechless, then his eyes trailed off to the field behind the trailer.

"That's why I can't stay."

Alice moved her head away from Gideon's shoulder. She looked up at him. He was still staring out into the field, his eyes scanning from right to left and back again. She thought of what he'd told her a long time ago, about the paths in life, and she wondered where they'd both end up. Gideon, he was searching like his road was in the field behind her trailer, but where did that road lead? Was he thinking of *her*, whoever he'd met, or was he thinking about Alice? He looked like he was thinking back, not looking forward. Alice didn't know what to make of that. All she really knew was that what Gideon had said almost hurt more than Ryan beating on her. It was worse, too, because she felt she deserved it.

She moved her body over, giving him space, and straightened her shirt out even though it was resting perfectly. What am I wearing? Blue jeans. Black shirt. Dirty camouflage sneakers. She owned one dress, if that, and never wore it. She never wanted to until that moment. She pushed her hair behind her ears, licked her lips, cleared her throat.

"What's her name?" Alice said.

"That don't matter, really. That's private," he ended up saying.

Alice turned away, not sure what to do or say. She wanted to know the woman's name, and more. What was it about her that made him want to stay in the city, a place he'd never cared for, rather than be with Alice and the girls? She wanted to tell him to fuck off for saying that. But things between them were already so strained. She was hurt. He was hurt. If they had anything, maybe it was that. The hurt. What else was there?

She looked around aimlessly as though there were answers in the gravel at her feet, in the rust at the bottom of the truck's passenger door, hidden under the rocks she'd piled up. And then she remembered the paper Jayne had given her, clutched firmly in her hand. She carefully unfolded it to reveal a picture, and she nudged Gideon to look at it with her.

It showed the back of Alice's house. Alice recognized the girls' swing set, the tire swing, the big open field, and the trees in the distance. Kathy and Jayne were standing at the front of the field right beside a woman she could only guess was herself, she being dressed in a very familiar pair of blue jeans and a black shirt. Grace was in the sky beside a couple of M-shaped birds and a bright yellow sun that had sunglasses on. Grace had wings. Beside Alice, there was another figure, a man. Alice didn't know who it was.

"Want to call Jayne over here?" Alice said to Gideon, without looking up from the picture.

Gideon called to Jayne, who came running.

"Didja like it?" she said, hopping up and down in anticipation.

"I love it," Alice said and then pointed at the man. "But, who is this right here? Is this the angel you girls met?"

"No," Jayne said to her mother.

"Who is it then? Your daddy?" Gideon said.

"No," Jayne said. "It's you, silly."

Alice watched as Jayne threw her arms around Gideon, and he picked her up and twirled her around, squeezing her as tight as he dared. When he placed her down, she gave him a quick peck on the cheek before darting off to return to her game with Kathy. He was left smiling wide with pink cheeks. When he looked over at Alice, she handed him the picture.

"The girls need you," she said.

Gideon looked at the picture carefully, and his smile didn't fade. That's when Alice realized that it wasn't just the girls who needed him. She did too.

"You can keep the picture," she said.

"Yeah?" Gideon said.

"I don't think Jayne would mind," Alice said. "I don't mind."

Gideon nodded. He folded up the picture and slid it into his pocket.

"You know, maybe I can stay for a little bit," he said.

From the truck at the side of the highway, Alice called out to her girls.

"Darlings, why don't you go play around back."

"In the field?" Kathy said.

"Yes," she said. "In the field."

They screeched in delight and disappeared behind the trailer. Alice and Gideon walked in that direction. They navigated their way through all the toys in the driveway and went around back, ending up at the tire swing. Alice got on and Gideon stood by her side. She held the yellow twine tightly in her hands and began to pump her legs.

EPILOGUE

On the day that Kathy couldn't sleep, the sun was setting reluctantly, splashing red and yellow and orange across the horizon and painting the walls of the girls' bedroom. Kathy always liked how the sunset cast colours against her walls, when it came in clear like it did tonight, when the Dora blanket on the bedroom window was pushed over to the side. She thought it was pretty how the colours moved like liquid against the walls as though she were inside a lava lamp. She'd been watching the light for a good while now and didn't want it to leave. She didn't want the night to come, or the sun to set. She knew it was only a matter of time, however, and that made her sad, and she started to cry. At that moment, Alice walked by on the way to her own bedroom. She stopped at the girls' bedroom door.

"Kathy, is that you? Are you awake?" Alice said.

"I can't sleep," she said.

Alice walked over to Kathy and Jayne's mattress, which rested in the middle of the bedroom. She sat down at Kathy's side and wiped some tears away from her cheek. Jayne groaned and rolled over on her side. She never had much trouble sleeping, that one. Not so long as there was a warm body for her to cuddle against.

"What's wrong, darling?" Alice said.

Kathy hesitated only for a moment. She took her mother's hand.

"Are you afraid of dying?" Kathy said.

Alice squeezed her hand.

"Sure I am. Of course I am, sometimes," Alice said.

Kathy looked away from her mother, to the bedroom walls. The colours were still moving across her walls like flames. They were dimmer now, though. They weren't as vibrant as they were even a few minutes ago. The sun would be gone soon.

"Am I going to die?' Kathy said.

Alice sighed. She squeezed Kathy's hand even tighter.

"One day you'll die. One day everybody on this earth will die," Alice said.

Kathy cried some more. Alice wiped away more tears.

"Why?" Kathy said.

"I don't know, honey," Alice said. "I don't know the answer to that. It's just the way things are. At least we're all in the same boat. I feel good about that sometimes."

The room had grown much darker by now. The red and yellow and orange had been painted over by grey and black.

"Do you think you can sleep? Do you want me to stay?" Alice said.

Kathy pulled at her mother's hand. Alice lay down beside her. She took Kathy into her arms and covered her like a blanket. Kathy opened her eyes and closed her eyes and saw the same thing either way.

"Mommy, will I wake up tomorrow?" Kathy said.

"Yes," Alice said. "That's one thing I know for sure."

ACKNOWLEDGMENTS

Throughout the process of writing *The Evolution of Alice,* many people have helped me, inspired me, and supported me.

Warren Cariou was there right from the beginning, when *Alice* was just one short story. Warren has been much more than an editor to me. He's been a friend, a mentor, a sounding board, and a fan. I'm a better writer because of him.

Penny Thomas's incredible and haunting stories served as inspiration for some of the (perhaps) supernatural events in the novel. And whenever I asked if she had more ghost stories, she usually did.

My wife, Jill, gave me time to work on this novel. She's my best friend and greatest supporter. And my children have always inspired me to create a better world through my writing.

Cam, Mike, and Dad have provided lifelong support, but it was my mom's unwavering belief in me that often kept me believing in myself. I still remember, at eight, telling her that I was going to write a book one day; she never told me otherwise.

My publisher, Highwater Press, always supports my work and is like a second family to me.

Thanks also to the Manitoba Arts Council for their support.

Finally, I want to acknowledge the First Nations community that served as the inspiration for this novel. It is a place of beauty, where one person is tied to another, one family is tied to another, and they celebrate together and they grieve together, and I wish we were all like that, because nothing should ever happen in a vacuum. Not writing or anything else.

ABOUT THE AUTHOR

David Alexander Robertson is the creator of several graphic novels, including his newest series, Tales from Big Spirit, as well as the bestselling 7 Generations series. He was a contributor to the anthology *Manitowapow: Aboriginal Writings from the Land of Water* (2012) and is co-creator and writer for the upcoming television series *The Reckoner*. David lives in Winnipeg with his family, where he works in the field of indigenous education.